Joyful
Encounters

Kathleen McKee

Joyful Encounters is a work of fiction. Names, characters, and incidents were created by the author's imagination or are used fictitiously. To my knowledge, there is no Monastery of St. Carmella. Any similarity of persons or locales is purely coincidental.

First Edition: March 2016
Revised: January 2019

Cover design by Robin Ludwig Design Inc.
www.gobookcoverdesign.com

ISBN-10: 1540308146
ISBN-13: 978-1540308146

Printed in the United States of America

.

"According to Vedanta, there are only two... indications that a transformation is taking place within you... The first symptom is that you... become light-hearted and full of joy. The second symptom is that you encounter more and more meaningful coincidences in your life... And this accelerates to the point where you actually experience the miraculous."

— Deepak Chopra

Also by Kathleen McKee

The Poustinia Series:
. Poustinia: A Novel
Joyful Encounters
Bountiful Legacies

A Specter of Truth

Living with a Springer Spaniel:
Pete and Me

No Gifts to Bring

Recipes of some of the foods prepared in *Joyful Encounters* are available at https://kathleen-mckee.com/category/recipes/

Chapter 1

I was proud of Amanda as she walked across the platform to receive her culinary arts diploma. She looked self-confident and poised, a far cry from the bedraggled ragamuffin I had met last June during a fierce thunder storm. At center stage, she turned to the audience and gave a winning smile. We all cheered loudly, knowing that she'd overcome many challenges to reach her goal.

Amanda Angeli is an attractive young woman, now 19 years of age. She's of petite build, with iridescent brown eyes and long brown hair. When I first encountered Amanda at a cabin in the woods at the Monastery of St. Carmella, she was going through a rather rebellious stage. Neon streaked hair and numerous body piercings made her appear to be more like a street punk or rock star. Neither is the case any longer.

I, too, have had a transformation this year. I attributed it to my experiences at the monastery, and my interactions with the people I met there. Initially, I booked a week's stay at the rustic cabin—a poustinia—to discern whether I should retire from my VP position at a publishing firm in the city. I haven't yet made any decision about that. I figure I'll know what to do when the time is right.

At the graduation ceremony, I sat between Amanda's dad and her grandfather, Charlie Munley. Amanda also invited her aunt, Sister Tony, to the Commencement. It was only this past

Thanksgiving that we learned the family connection that bound each of them together. The three of them have become my good friends. I reflected on those bonds as Amanda crossed the stage.

Charlie's the resident groundskeeper at the Monastery of St. Carmella. He's been there for about 10 years, ever since he reunited with his deceased wife's sister, Sister Tony. Charlie and Sister Tony had the brilliant idea to build five poustinias on the grounds of the monastery. The rustic cabins would be a source of revenue for the Sisters, and a place of solitude for guests.

I learned about the poustinias from a brochure I found at my local post office. Although I was somewhat hesitant to spend a week alone in the woods, I was enticed by the opportunity to bask in the serenity of nature. The fact that there was a lake and vineyard at the monastery was very alluring. Little did I know that the experience would be so life-changing.

Amanda stayed in the cabin next to mine during that June week last summer. She didn't choose to be there. Rather, her dad thought that a poustinia might be a safe retreat, away from the influence of her dysfunctional friends. Misguided as it may have been, Steve Angeli was only trying to protect his daughter. After the death of Amanda's mother, he struggled to know how to handle a headstrong teen.

In a short time, I began to see Amanda's strengths, and recognized that she might thrive in an environment of support and empowerment. My firm offered her a temporary clerical position, and I invited Amanda to live with me for the summer. It wasn't an easy decision for Steve, but he gave his approval.

My neighbor, Myra, and her family were also attending the graduation ceremony. Myra's granddaughter, Kate, was the one who got Amanda interested in attending culinary school. They enrolled in the same academic program, and they shared an apartment near school.

Amanda and Kate have become the best of friends. It was Myra who introduced Kate to Amanda, and Myra who tried to teach me a little about the psychology you need to use when you're sharing your space, as I did, with a young adult like Amanda. I learned a lot from her. Meaning Myra. But I have to say that I learned a lot from Amanda, too.

Joe Henderson is another culinary classmate, and a close friend of Amanda and Kate. Joe had a rough childhood and got into some trouble with the law. A compassionate judge gave him probation but required him to do community service at a soup kitchen. He worked himself up from pot washer to line cook and discovered that he enjoyed being a chef. The priest in charge of the soup kitchen, Father Jim, recognized Joe's talents, offering him a full scholarship to culinary school.

Just before Amanda started school last fall, she learned that she was pregnant. An unfortunate liaison with her drug addicted former boyfriend the previous spring was unsettling to say the least, but she was determined to keep her baby. Sadly, Addison Victoria died *in utero* from an undetected congenital birth defect. Amanda acknowledged that Kate, Joe, and Father Jim helped her get through a very difficult time in her life.

Joe's mother and Father Jim were also at the graduation ceremony. I hadn't met Joe's mother. Years of abusing alcohol had a disastrous impact on her spirit, but Father Jim has taken her under his wing. He's a licensed counselor, in addition to overseeing the soup kitchen and a homeless shelter in the city. Joe's mom now volunteers at the shelter and has been clean for nearly 5 months.

We cheered when Kate, and then Joe, also crossed the stage to receive their diplomas. Charlie squeezed my hand and whispered to me how proud he was of Amanda. I nodded my agreement, recognizing that neither of us had expected such a connection to these young adults at this stage of our lives.

We also didn't anticipate our own budding relationship, such as it is. I should speak for myself, being quite content with my living arrangements. My dog, Harvey, is good company.

Charlie, on the other hand, lives in one of the monastery poustinias. You might say that he was a loner, enjoying his quiet haven. But he and I hit it off.

Something's definitely brewing between us.

Chapter 2

After the commencement ceremony, we all went to dinner at the soup kitchen. I know it doesn't sound too festive, but Father Jim invited us, and it's what Amanda, Kate, and Joe wanted to do. Actually, I think it's rather fitting, because each of the graduates has an association there.

When we arrived at the graduation-themed dining room, I introduced myself to Joe's mother. I had a feeling she might feel somewhat awkward since she'd never met any of us.

"Hi, I'm Vicki Sullivan," I said with a welcoming smile.

"I'm Anne Henderson. Joe says good stuff about you."

"He's a fine young man. I know you must be very proud."

"I don't deserve such a good boy. It's mostly because of Father Jim. He's helped both of us."

Charlie joined us, and I introduced him to Anne. "Glad to meet you," he said, offering a handshake. Charlie's a man of few words until he gets to know you.

"Joe told me about you. He said you work at a monastery, and he's helped you a few times."

"Yep, Monastery of St. Carmella. Joe helped me with some of the spring clean-up on the grounds. Nice kid."

"Charlie's Amanda's grandfather," I noted. "The nun in charge of the monastery is around here somewhere. Sister Tony is Amanda's aunt." I scanned the crowd to see if I could find her.

"I met her before the graduation. She seems nice. Is she your sister, Charlie?"

"No, she's my wife's sister."

I explained that Charlie's wife, Stella, was killed in a car accident years ago. Their son, Steve, is Amanda's dad. As I was speaking, Joe joined us and gave his mother a hug.

"I'm glad you've met some of Amanda's family, mom. Now remember, you don't have to work today. We're here to celebrate."

"It don't seem right. Father Jim's working."

"No, he's not. He just went back to the kitchen to check on everything. He'll be joining us shortly."

I noticed that many of the crowd were beginning to seat themselves, and I invited Anne to sit next to me. The center of the dining room had been arranged by pushing several tables together to form a banquet table in the shape of a T. Amanda, Joe, and Kate, as the guests of honor, sat at the head of the table. Kate's family and Father Jim were asked to sit on the left side; Amanda's family and Joe's mother on the right.

All of the other tables in the dining room were set, as usual, for the regular guests of the soup kitchen. For this special occasion, each table had a paper tablecloth and a centerpiece of balloons. A large banner on the wall, and a beautifully decorated sheet cake on a table below it, proclaimed congratulations to the graduates.

I saw that Father Jim had returned to the dining room and was greeting each of the soup kitchen guests, most of them by name. He ushered in some of the stragglers standing hesitantly at the door, then joined the main table. Before he sat, Father Jim addressed the group.

"I'm happy that so many of you were able to join us today as we recognize the accomplishments of Joe, Kate, and Amanda. Not only did they achieve honors in their culinary arts program, but they've also shared their time and talents with us through their volunteer work at the shelter."

Everyone cheered, many quite exuberantly. After the hoots and whistles died down, Father Jim continued with a blessing of the food and those who had prepared it. That must have been the signal, because waiters began to present each of us with a plate of lasagna, green beans, and garlic bread. Others filled our glasses with water. I had a feeling that even the servers may have been regulars at the soup kitchen.

Myra sat directly across from me, and I introduced her to Joe's mother. I wasn't sure if Myra had yet met Joe, but she had certainly heard about him through me or her granddaughter, Kate.

Everyone should have a neighbor who is such a good friend. We often sit on each other's porch to chat when I get home from work. She also takes care of my dog, Harvey, if I decide to have a getaway at the monastery. Unfortunately, my schedule was a bit hectic this spring, and I only managed a few weekends staying in the rustic poustinia on the monastery grounds.

Each time I visited, Sister Tony took me through the wing of the mansion that was being renovated to house a Bed and Breakfast, gift shop, and restaurant. She's in charge of the poustinias, and I expect she'll also oversee any reservations for the B&B. It's exciting to see the progress, especially since Charlie and I orchestrated the fundraising for the Sisters.

While Myra and Anne chatted across the table, Charlie filled me in on some of the new developments at the monastery. We had just spoken on the phone the other night, but it seemed that progress on the B&B was occurring rapidly.

"The Sisters decided that the grand opening will be the second week of June," Charlie said. "We sent out a large mailing yesterday, so you should be getting an invitation soon. I've been posting flyers all over town."

"Wow, that's sooner than I expected. Can Amanda get all of the decorating done by then?"

Amanda had told me that Sister Tony hired her to be the chef and decorator for the restaurant and B&B. The Sisters offered her room and board at the B&B, as well as a small stipend, if she'd oversee the kitchen and guest facilities. In time, they hoped to be able to offer her a full salary.

Amanda was really excited about the opportunity to do the things she loves. She has an amazing talent for design, and she's an excellent chef. It's an added plus that Joe was hired as pastry chef at Jake's Diner in town. Amanda's happy that Joe will be living close by, and he plans to help her with the restaurant start-up. Kate decided to continue her studies and complete her bachelor's degree but promised to assist whenever she can.

"Tony said that Amanda's fine with the schedule," Charlie replied. "The furniture's arriving tomorrow, so she'll have about three weeks to settle in and get the rooms set up. Joe's going to rent a poustinia until he finds an apartment in town."

"What about the gift shop?"

"That still needs some work. We ordered a couple of glass display cabinets and a cash register, and we'll use the built-in bookcases, but it looks kind of empty. I thought maybe you and I could work on it if you can come to help next weekend."

"Definitely, if Myra can dog sit."

Myra's ears picked up when she heard her name. "It's not a problem for me to watch Harvey," she chirped. "You know he's always welcome."

Father Jim invited the three graduates to cut the cake, then the servers began to distribute it. I couldn't resist the tempting dessert and was lucky enough to get one of the icing flowers. Frosting's my favorite part of the cake.

I asked Charlie if he knew whether there would be a poustinia available for the weekend. It made me laugh when he said that he'd already booked it for me.

"Come to think of it," Charlie added, "we'd better make sure to reserve a poustinia for you during the grand opening—unless you're anticipating a stay at the B&B. You're planning to be there, aren't you?"

"Of course I am. I'll stay in a cabin so there's enough room for couples at the monastery B&B. I imagine Jeff and his wife will want to be there."

Jeff is CEO of a very successful business, and his company was a major contributor to the renovation fund for the Sisters. He's been coming to the poustinias for several years, but his wife wouldn't think of staying in a rustic cabin. They're now looking forward to booking a comfortable room in the B&B for both to enjoy the country ambiance.

"Tony said she's sure that some of the nuns from the midwest province will visit," Charlie noted, "but they can stay in the convent guest rooms. That's what she's calling the main part of the monastery for the Sisters' living space. The wing for the B&B is entirely separate now that the walls have been constructed."

I noticed that Amanda, Joe, and Kate were going from table to table to thank each of the guests for sharing in their celebration. By the time they got to us, Father Jim had joined them.

"I hear that Joe and Kate are helping Amanda move to the monastery B&B this week." he said to Sister Tony. "Her dad and I plan to lend a hand, if that's OK with you."

"That's great," Tony said. "I've been wondering when you might find the time to visit the Monastery of St. Carmella. Would you like me to reserve cabins for you and Steve?"

"We're not planning to stay overnight but thank you. I do want to make a private retreat at the end of the month, so I'll check my calendar and make the arrangements with you."

"Wonderful. We'd like you to offer Mass in the convent chapel while you're with us."

"Definitely. I'll be in touch."

Charlie and I stood to begin our rounds of farewells. I told Amanda that I'd give her a call in the morning as I handed her a graduation card. She put it in her purse, probably realizing there was money in it.

"Thanks so much, Vicki," she said. "You're awesome!"

When we met up with Steve, I said, "I'll be thinking of you as you help Amanda get settled this week. Isn't it amazing that a year ago you brought Amanda to the monastery to get her away from the friends she was hanging out with? Now she's returning by choice."

"I know. I still can't believe it."

"Amanda's new job will be good for her, although I pity the poor nuns," I said with a chuckle. "They won't know what hit them!"

When we reached the doorway, I turned and gave Charlie a kiss. "Keep me posted. I want to hear all about move-in day."

"I promise. Drive safe. I'll see you next weekend."

Chapter 3

I was able to leave work early on Friday afternoon in order to arrive at the monastery by supper time. Amanda had told me that Sister Tony wanted her to work on creating an affordable menu for the B&B restaurant, so Charlie, Joe, and I would be her first guinea pigs. She made sure we understood that we were to pay for our meals.

Charlie was pruning some trees along the winding drive of the Monastery of St. Carmella when I arrived. I pulled over and called out, "Don't you ever take a break?"

"Figured I'd do some work while I was waiting for you. I told Tony I'd take you to your poustinia so she can enjoy supper with the nuns tonight."

"Aren't we having dinner at the monastery?"

"Yeah, but the Sisters are having a get-together in their community room while we test Amanda's meal. We can drop off your stuff at the cabin first, and you can freshen up. The golf cart's in the parking lot."

"OK, hop in my car. I'll drive us there."

After I parked, Charlie loaded my bags into the golf cart and took me to the closest poustinia. It was the cabin I'd stayed in during my first visit to the monastery.

"I thought this poustinia was reserved for the newbies," I said as Charlie retrieved my things.

"We don't have any guests other than Joe this weekend. Thought you might enjoy the proximity of this one."

All of the cabins are identical. As you open the door, you see a single bed and nightstand. To the left of the doorway is a window, under which is a small writing desk and chair. To the right is a little kitchenette with a single cook top, microwave, and mini-refrigerator. Just beyond that is a small bathroom with a shower, toilet, and pedestal sink. The front porch boasts two rocking chairs and a little side table.

I threw my purse on the bed and used the powder room while Charlie brought in my suitcase and the bag of groceries. I didn't bring too much food. Just some tea bags and snacks since I was only staying the weekend. Besides, Amanda said we'd be having our meals at the monastery.

In a matter of minutes, I joined Charlie in the golf cart, smiling at the memory of my first ride to the poustinia with Sister Tony. I had been somewhat wary that day last summer. Now I was excited to be back.

Charlie and I chatted on our return to the front entrance of the monastery. I asked if the Sisters had selected a name for the restaurant yet.

"Everyone's been making suggestions, but no decisions have been made. I figure we can talk about it at dinner. Amanda wants your input."

"What about Sister Tony and the other nuns? Don't they want to decide?"

"Yeah, they'll make the final decision after we give them our list."

Charlie pulled up to the monastery's *porte couchère* and parked the golf cart. As he opened the ornate front door of the mansion, a bell tinkled our arrival. Amanda met us by the grand staircase in the front hall.

"You made good time," Amanda said, as she gave me a hug. "Joe's in the kitchen. We can head to the dining room."

I noticed that two new bathrooms had been added on the left, just beyond the stairs. Attractive placards on the doors identified one for men and one for women.

"Good thinking," I said to Charlie. "We forgot about main floor bathrooms in our planning."

"The architect we hired added them into the design. He was able to use the space from one of the parlors. Can't have guests dining at the restaurant or visiting the gift shop without providing restrooms."

"That's true. Isn't there another parlor?"

"Yeah. It was repurposed to be a sitting room for those staying at the B&B. We moved furniture from Tony's office for seating and hung the large screen TV that Jeff Stodges donated on the wall. Looks pretty good."

I took a peek inside and agreed that it appeared inviting. A sofa, love seat, and two Queen Anne chairs, as well as a couple of recliners were strategically placed. I thought it was a nice idea to include a game table in the corner. The ornate chess set on top provided an attractive, yet functional, display.

As we continued down the hallway, I saw that the right corridor by the elevator was blocked by a newly constructed wall. I was surprised to see an attractive pocket door leading to the nuns' quarters.

Raising my eyebrows, I remarked, "I thought there'd be no entrance to the convent from this wing."

"The architect suggested it to the nuns in case they want easy access to the restaurant or gift shop. If you look closely, you'll see a keypad lock hidden in the molding. Only the Sisters have the code."

"Very clever. I like it."

We entered the dining room on the left, and I noted that Amanda had already been working to make the nuns' refectory look like a real restaurant. There was even a small counter by the door with a point-of-sales register.

The Sisters hadn't needed to purchase new tables or chairs. Instead, Amanda arranged twelve tables-for-four around the room. Each was decorated with a washable pink tablecloth and a tea light centerpiece. She had lit the little candle at the table we were to have our dinner.

"This looks lovely, Amanda," I said as I gazed around the room. "Nice job!"

"Thanks. It's not done yet. But it's a start. We can push tables together if we get larger groups."

I nodded my approval, imagining the elegant soirees and dinner parties of the wealthy couple who originally built the mansion. Eventually, the Sisters converted it to a more simply furnished refectory, devoid of any ostentation.

"I think it still needs some plants," Amanda continued, "and Aunt Tony said I could switch out some of the religious pictures on the wall. I told her I didn't think the Last Supper portrait would fit in with my design."

"You might want to think that through a little more," I suggested. "After all, it's a monastery restaurant."

"Yeah, but it's not part of the convent. Anyway, it's a work in progress. Have a seat while I check on Joe."

With the flourish of a butler, Charlie pulled out a chair for me. He does have some endearing qualities, I thought as he sat to my right.

Chapter 4

The menu for tonight's supper was printed on a sheet of paper at each place setting. The price was unobtrusively added at the bottom of the page. Apparently, we were having a garden salad with house vinaigrette, 4 oz. rib eye steak, twice-baked potato, and roasted mixed vegetables. Dessert was chocolate toffee mousse.

Amanda returned with a basket of warm rolls and a plate of butter pats, saying that the salad would be served in a second. "Hey GP, how do you like your steak cooked?" she asked.

Charlie laughed at my questioning look. "That's what Amanda decided to call me. It's short for grandpop, or so she says."

"Medium's fine with me."

"Me, too," I said, chuckling at the GP thing.

Before long, Amanda and Joe brought salads for each of us. After serving, they joined Charlie and me at the table.

"Good to see you again, Joe," I said. "Looks like you're Amanda's right-hand man."

"We make a good team. Too bad the nuns can't afford both of us. At least not until they see if the restaurant can make a go of it."

"Have you started work at Jake's Diner yet?"

"Yeah, I began on Tuesday. I like it. It's nice that it's a day job since they want me to make desserts for the supper crowd. Then I can come over here and help Amanda with her menus. We're planning to be up and running for the grand opening."

"Is Jake angry with the nuns for starting the restaurant? He was the only gig in town."

"Nah, he's cool with it. Said the town needed a nice place for special occasions. He's been giving me some pointers, like we shouldn't offer too many menu options all at once."

"That sounds like good advice. Are you thinking about *a la carte* or a fixed price for your meals?"

"We're doing fixed price tonight. Mostly because we're not giving you any choice for your meal, and we want to test out a dessert item. But when we open, we'll do both. Like, customers can get an entrée that includes a starch and veggies for one price, then salads and desserts are extra."

"That's pretty typical."

"Yeah, Jake said he makes more profit doing it that way. He let us use his recipe for the mousse. It's not a big seller at his place. Most people order the pies. He thinks maybe the mousse would be more popular at a fancier restaurant."

"I think you should still offer pie here," Charlie said. We all laughed, knowing that Charlie always ordered pie when he went to the diner.

"Gotcha, GP," Amanda replied with a wink to the rest of us. "Make a list of your favorite pies, and that's what we'll focus on."

As we finished our salads, Amanda and Joe took our dishes to the kitchen and brought out the entrée plates. The food was attractively arranged and looked delicious.

"This is definitely a winner," I said as I took a bite of the tender, juicy steak smothered with sautéed mushrooms and onions. I noticed that Charlie didn't even ask for the ketchup.

"So, what are your thoughts about the name of the restaurant?" I asked, reaching for a roll.

"I was thinking that *Monastery Restaurant* would be a good name," Charlie said. "That's what everyone in town's going to call it anyway."

"No way!" Amanda exclaimed. "That's so lame."

"How about *Vineyard Lodge and Fine Dining*?" Joe asked.

"Remember, the Sisters will decide," I said. "Put it on the list, but so far I'm not crazy about either of the suggestions. I do like the idea of bringing the vineyards into the name. What do you think of *Vintner's Garden*?"

Amanda asked, "What the heck is a vintner?"

"It's a person who makes wine."

"Yeah, but we're not making wine here. Guess you could put it on the list for the nuns. The garden idea's cool. I'd like to focus on the farm-to-table theme. That's pretty popular right now."

"How about *Garden Tea Room*?" I asked as Joe brought us our desserts. I guess by now everyone knew I enjoyed my tea.

"It doesn't grab me," Amanda said. "How do you like the mousse?"

"Love it," I said. "I think it should be a menu item. It's light and airy, yet still decadent. Very nice." Charlie agreed, but said he'd still prefer pie.

"Are we going to test more meals tomorrow?" I asked.

"Yeah," Joe said. "We're planning a brunch buffet around 11 a.m. We invited the Sisters, if any of them want to join us. Kate's coming for the day, and she'll help serve and clean up. Then, we'll have supper at 6:30 p.m. for the five of us."

"Sounds good to me," I said. "I think Charlie and I are going to be working in the gift shop."

"Yep. Thought we could meet there around 9:30 a.m. Is that OK for you?"

"It's perfect. Now I think we should help clean up the kitchen, so these two waifs can do something fun."

"Not much to do around here on a Friday night," Joe said. "Besides, I think we're going to start prepping for tomorrow."

"Oh, my gosh! It's Friday night and Charlie's supposed to call Bingo at the firehouse," I exclaimed.

"No problem," Charlie said. "I made arrangements with one of my buddies. Told him we'd be testing recipes for the new restaurant tonight. Figured the more people who knew about it, the more business I could drum up."

"Good thinking, GP," Amanda noted as she began clearing the table. We helped her bring the dinnerware to the kitchen, and Joe loaded the dishwasher. After everything was cleaned up, Amanda took us to the register kiosk and entered the sales.

"We take all major credit cards, so cough it up."

After we paid, I said, "Do you need any help in the kitchen tonight?"

"Nah, we're OK."

Charlie turned to me and said, "Then I challenge you to a game of chess."

"I haven't played chess in years."

"Good. That means I'll win."

Chapter 5

Saturday morning dawned clear, but chilly. Putting on a sweater, I took my mug of tea to the front porch of the cabin. I loved watching the different varieties of birds and tried to identify them by their colorful plumage or the sound of their songs.

I'd have to get Charlie's help on the ones not familiar to me. He's a bird aficionado and builds amazing birdhouses in his spare time. He's been trying to teach me about their various calls and the types of food they enjoy.

Last evening was enjoyable, I thought, even though I was easily defeated in chess. Supper was elegant, and the menu was a nice choice for an upscale restaurant. Still, I wondered how far the food budget would stretch. Neither Amanda nor Joe were experienced chefs, and they both had limited knowledge of the business side of running a restaurant.

Jake's been quite honorable in giving Joe some pointers, while Sister Tony's an astute business woman. She knows how to monitor expenses and use available resources. Those skills will be helpful, but it's not going to be easy to make a go of it.

A particularly active squirrel caught my attention. It scurried among the trees clutching a nut in its front teeth like a jackal with its prey. I thought about Sister Tony and wondered how she was handling all of the challenges of construction, as well as planning for the grand opening in only a few weeks. While the Sisters had been supportive of converting a wing of the mansion to a B&B as a revenue source, this must be a very stressful time for them.

It was quite unusual for Tony to not be available when I arrived, but even stranger that she didn't pop in to see how the first menu offering was progressing. I reminded myself to ask Charlie if she was doing OK.

My reverie was interrupted when I realized the time. I brought my mug into the cabin, made the bed, and freshened up. I was ready to begin our day's work in the gift shop.

∧∧∧

Charlie was waiting for me at the front entrance when I arrived at the monastery. I noticed that he had lugged dozens of cartons from who knows where and had begun to open them. His face lit up as he said, "Morning, Vicki. Perfect timing!"

"Hi, Charlie. Looks like you started already. What's in the boxes?"

"I brought some cases of wine and Julie's jellies from the basement. Also, the nuns ordered wholesale items that we can sell. I added some of the birdhouses I made through the winter."

"Wonderful! Where do you want me to start?"

"Let's open more boxes. We need to see how the nuns want to arrange the displays before we start placing the items. Dolores is going to be in charge of the gift shop, and Julie will be her assistant. They should be here any minute."

Sister Dolores and Sister Julie had been at the monastery for a number of years. They're both in their early sixties and teach English as a Second Language to migrant workers at a nearby farm. They had their initial training at the monastery, then they'd been assigned to teach at the local school in town.

Now that they're semi-retired, they assist Sister Tony with her duties at the monastery.

"I hope they got some hats and sunscreen," I said. "Those were things I had never thought to pack on my first visit to the poustinia last year."

"If they didn't, there's still time to order some. Tony said she didn't want to go overboard. Money's getting tight."

"Speaking of Tony, where is she? She's usually in the thick of things."

"She's around. In fact, she stopped in shortly before you arrived. I think she plans to be at the brunch."

"Did Kate arrive yet?"

"Yeah. She's in the kitchen with Amanda and Joe."

Dolores appeared at the door with two large bags. After greeting Charlie and me, she told us that the older Sisters in the infirmary had been making lap afghans and knitted scarves to sell in the gift shop. Though she wasn't sure how popular they'd be, she didn't want to disappoint them by not adding the items to their inventory.

I thought Dolores seemed a little flustered. She told me that she was glad the construction work in the monastery is just about complete. I could identify, having experienced the turmoil of my kitchen remodel a few years ago. Still, that was minor compared to all of the work being done in the living space for the nuns.

"Guess we should position the display counters before we do anything else," Dolores said. "I drew a floor plan to guide us. I also want Tony's office desk moved to the left of the door, so we can put the cash register on it."

Luckily the furniture slid pretty easily across the carpet with the three of us working together. Once the counters and desk were positioned, Dolores suggested that Charlie and I start placing bottles of wine on the built-in bookshelves.

We all greeted Julie when she arrived. Dolores asked her to start shelving her jellies.

"Not so fast," Julie said. "I made these classy little stickers for the tops of the jars, and I bought ribbon to tie a bow around them."

Dolores rolled her eyes and said, "You couldn't have done that before today?"

I could see that all of the recent commotion was causing taut nerves. Sister Julie didn't seem fazed by Dolores' comment.

"Don't worry. I'll stay out of your way, and work on my jelly jars as I put them on the shelf in the corner."

Charlie lugged in a chair from the sitting room for Julie, then carried in two boxes of grape jelly from the hallway so she could begin decorating the jars. When one was finished, she held it up for all of us to see. "Don't you think this is cute?"

"I love it," I said, wanting to be supportive. "I think your jellies will be a popular item in the gift shop."

Back to task, I handed Charlie some more wine bottles to shelve. "Does the monastery need a liquor license to sell these?" I asked.

"We had an off-premises license," Dolores replied. "We had to apply for an on-premises license. That will allow us to sell wine in the gift shop and the restaurant. We're good to go now."

Everything was so much more complicated than I had expected. No wonder Tony had been hesitant about our idea of a B&B.

Charlie asked me to continue shelving the wine, while he set up the display of his birdhouses. Dolores was arranging the nuns' handcrafted items. We were working in a good rhythm when Amanda arrived to say that brunch was ready.

It was perfect timing.

Chapter 6

A buffet table was set up along the side wall of the dining room. Three chafing pans held scrambled eggs, bacon, and pancakes. Buttered toast points, coffee cake, and tea sandwiches were on platters, and condiments were placed next to them. Charlie and I seated ourselves, and we were joined by Dolores and Julie. I was happy to see Sister Tony arrive. She sat with Kate, Amanda, and Joe.

Amanda welcomed us and explained that today's brunch was a fixed price menu. She noted that we were permitted to return for seconds. Beverages would be an additional cost and include coffee, tea, and orange juice. Water was complimentary.

I greeted Kate and Sister Tony as I joined the buffet line. Tony gave me a hug, and said she was happy to see me again. I asked if any of the other Sisters would be coming to brunch.

"Not today," Tony said. "The Sisters in the infirmary were served breakfast after Mass this morning. I agreed to the brunch because Amanda's trying to determine what would be feasible for the B&B. How's the gift shop coming along?"

"We're making progress. We got the counters arranged where Dolores wants them, so now we're able to place the items for sale. Once we empty all of the boxes, I guess we'll have to figure out prices."

Sister Tony promised to stop by the gift shop after our meal. She said she was concerned that the shelves might look too sparse, but she had confidence in Dolores' ability to manage the place. Returning to our respective tables, I was embarrassed about my full plate, but I knew the chefs wanted feedback about each item on the menu.

As we ate, Amanda served each of us the beverage of our choice. I wondered if she was feeling overwhelmed, though she certainly didn't seem stressed. I was pleased that her friends were helping. They've been a good support.

When we finished our meal, Tony told us that she had a few announcements. She stood between the two tables and had our rapt attention.

"First, I'd like to thank you for your input on the name for the B&B and restaurant. The Sisters and I want to retain our identity and keep everything simple. We've decided to call our new enterprise the *Monastery Restaurant and Inn.*"

Amanda didn't look very happy about the Sisters' choice. She scrunched her nose and gave a side glance to Joe.

"I've also received some rather surprising news," Tony continued. "I've been elected to the administrative council for our merger with the mid-west province. I'll be moving to St. Louis, where I'll begin my new ministry on the first of July. The Sisters are aware of this development, and they've taken on a number of responsibilities for the start-up of the restaurant, B&B, and gift shop."

I was in shock and could see similar reactions on the faces of Amanda, Kate, and Joe. Amanda was the first to respond.

"You can't be serious," she said. "Don't they know that you run this place? I mean like you've been here forever. Tell them you don't want the job."

"I take a vow of obedience, Amanda. I have to go. But don't worry. Dolores and Julie will be fully involved, and the community's sending a replacement for me."

"We don't want someone new."

"You'll like Sister Marian. She's young, and she's excited to be a part of our new ministry here. In fact, she'll be arriving in time for the grand opening. I know that you'll make her feel welcome."

Amanda muttered something under her breath and began clearing the table. I knew better than to try to soften the blow. Anything I said would be held against me. Besides, I was pretty upset myself.

Charlie and I helped carry our dishes to the kitchen when the Sisters departed. Amanda and her friends insisted that they didn't need any further assistance. I left money on the table to cover the cost of my meal before joining Charlie to return to the gift shop. We were both lost in our thoughts.

I tried to compose myself as we continued our shelving tasks. None of us spoke about Tony's news but it was like an elephant in the room. Instead, Tony said she liked the furniture arrangement, and she made some additional suggestions for the displays. She helped to unpack a carton of religious items that seemed appropriate for a monastery, and I assisted Julie with the jelly jar decorating. Charlie began breaking down boxes, then took them to the trash bin out back.

We were finished by late afternoon. The gift shop looked pretty good despite the somewhat meager inventory. We all agreed that it needed some sundries and snack items, which Dolores told us she'd purchase for the grand opening.

The Sisters thanked me for my help, and Charlie said he'd head out with me. I assured Tony of my prayers as Charlie and I walked with her to the door.

"I guess I have the same sentiments as Amanda," I said to Sister Tony, "but I'm also aware that this new assignment will enable you to ensure the continued success of the Monastery of St. Carmella."

"This move is difficult for me, Vicki. Quite honestly, I don't want to go. I've shed many tears in our chapel, praying for the strength to handle such a change. Still, it's part of the calling that I received many years ago, and I believe that I must be open to the direction of God's plan."

"You sure they wouldn't let you do the administrative work here? Lots of companies now offer positions that can be done remotely."

"I'm positive," Tony replied with a firm nod of her head. "Promise me that you'll help Amanda adjust to the news. I want the grand opening to be a success."

"That's easier said than done," I said. "But don't worry. She'll come around in her own good time."

^^^

"I'm sorry that Tony's news came as such a shock," Charlie said as we took the shaded path to my cabin. "She asked us not to tell anyone until she was ready."

"I understand. I guess I just never expected that she'd be reassigned."

"This is a rough time for her. But don't worry. She'll make sure everything's in order before she leaves."

"I know she will, but it's not going to be the same without her."

We walked along in silence, both of us considering the ramifications of Tony's move to St. Louis. When we got to my porch, Charlie plopped down on one of the rocking chairs. I sat in the other one and told Charlie that I knew the news was difficult for him as well.

Charlie nodded in agreement, his expression one of deep consternation. "I don't know what to do."

"What's not to know? You think you'd be evicted when the new boss arrives?"

"Tony says no, but it's more than that. This has been my home for 10 years. I finally found peace when Tony took me in and let me work on the grounds. I have no doubt in my mind that Stella led me here, led me to Tony."

"So you're thinking that Stella would want you to follow Tony to St. Louis?"

"Yeah."

"Did you tell Tony?"

"Yeah."

"What'd she say?"

"She didn't think it was a good idea."

I had never heard anything so ridiculous in my life, but I knew that I needed to tread softly. This was obviously a huge dilemma for Charlie.

"I understand that Tony was instrumental in helping you through a rough time. But I think I know you well enough to say that you find solace in tranquility, in nature. This place has been good for you. Perhaps Stella led you here to the monastery, not to Tony."

"No, she led me to Tony. I have to go to St. Louis."

"Think this through, Charlie," I said, trying not to show my dismay. "You've recently reconnected with your son, Steve, and discovered that Amanda's your granddaughter. Do you really want to leave them?"

"No, but I have to be with Tony."

"So, what's Tony going to do? Arrive at her new place with you in tow and tell the nuns they have to find a job for you?"

"I don't know."

"And I hate to bring this up," I said, "but what about us?"

Charlie gazed at me, deep sadness in his eyes. Then he shook his head and slowly rose from his chair to depart.

In barely a whisper he said, "I have to be with Tony."

Chapter 7

I was still in turmoil as I drove home on Sunday morning. Mostly I was kicking myself for being such a sentimental old fool. Quite honestly, I'd developed feelings for Charlie but, obviously, they were misguided.

We had been a morose table of four at last evening's menu planning supper. Charlie never showed, and Amanda was a grump. Regardless, the meal was delicious. We had a seafood combo of jumbo shrimp and mussels, with broccoli and cherry tomatoes in a garlic wine sauce, served on a bed of linguini. Caesar salad was the appetizer, and cream puffs were the dessert.

Joe explained that they had decided on five dinner items that would be suitable for fine dining. These included the steak entrée we had last night, as well as chicken picante, broiled salmon, the seafood combo with linguini, and a vegetarian option.

All of them could be made to order rather easily and would be affordable. Leftovers could be made into soups *du jour*, and specials would be added based on season availability. Amanda planned to initially print menus for daily use, until she saw which items were the most popular.

Besides discussing the menus, we mostly spoke about Tony's departure. I didn't mention Charlie's dilemma. That would have sent Amanda over the edge. She had only recently learned that Charlie was her grandfather, and she was just beginning to enjoy the comfort of his attention and support.

Joe and Kate tried to tease Amanda out of her bad mood, but they also knew that she had to work through the process of acceptance. That's just how she is.

As for me, I was disgruntled in my own right. A night of tossing and turning didn't help matters. The more I considered Charlie's decision to follow Tony, the more irritated I got. If he thought I was going to beg him to stay, he was wrong.

I should have known better than to develop an emotional tie with someone so different from me. I've been perfectly content with my single status. At least for the most part.

I picked up Harvey from Myra's house and we chatted a while on her porch. I'm not sure if she detected my negative disposition. If she did, she kept it to herself. Myra's good at using psychology.

Instead, I told her about the menu planning meals, and how Kate spent the day helping Amanda and Joe in the kitchen. "It was so nice to see the three of them working together. They love creating new recipes and tasty food."

"I have a feeling that Kate will be spending her free time at the monastery," Myra said. "Now that the nuns are starting a restaurant, she's going to want to be involved."

"I know. The girls have mentioned that they wanted their own establishment. This'll be a good experience for them."

"Yeah, that's why Kate's continuing on to get a business degree. Without a doubt, it'll help her understand the financial aspects of operating a kitchen."

"I was a little worried that Amanda would be in over her head with the new start-up. Luckily, the guy who owns the diner in town has been giving Joe a lot of good advice. I also figured that Sister Tony's business skills would keep them afloat. Only problem is, Tony just got transferred."

"Oh, no! Isn't she Amanda's aunt?"

"Yeah, the news came as a big surprise this weekend. Amanda was pretty upset."

"That sounds like a dumb move. Aren't they opening the B&B shortly?"

"Yep, two more weeks. They're sending a replacement. Some young nun who's probably still wet behind the ears. I'm staying out of it."

"That'll be the day," Myra said. We both chuckled as I gathered Harvey's stuff and led him home.

^ ^ ^

I made myself a cup of hot tea and tried to read the newspaper. Every few moments I'd lose my focus, and my thoughts would reinforce my irritation. I decided to call Betty Sweeney, a gal I'd met on my first visit to the monastery.

Betty's a public defender, and she likes to unwind in the rustic location. We've become pretty good friends. In fact, she and I often make poustinia reservations at the same time, so we can catch up with one another. Betty has a way of seeing the positive in every situation, and she gives good advice.

"I was just thinking about calling you," Betty said as she answered the phone.

"Mental telepathy. You must have known I'm in a bad mood."

"Uh oh. Problems at work?"

"Not this time. I've been jilted--again."

Betty knew about Kenny, the man I had thought I would marry long ago. Unfortunately, he took a job on the west coast and forged a new life for himself.

"What? Charlie left you?"

"He's planning on it."

I told Betty about my weekend at the monastery, and the recent events of Tony's transfer to St. Louis. She gasped at the news but listened without interrupting as I told my tale of woe.

"He wants to be with Tony," I said with sorrowful sigh.

"That's ridiculous!"

"I know. That's what I think."

"Tell him how you feel."

"I did. Well, sort of. It doesn't matter. He believes that Stella led him to Tony, and the peace he's found is due to her."

"Can nuns do that? Bring a guy with them when they're transferred?"

"I don't know. I mean he's her brother-in-law. It's not like there's something going on between them."

"It never seemed like it to me. Is Tony encouraging him?"

"No. Charlie said she doesn't like the idea."

"What about Steve and Amanda? Gosh, Charlie just found his long-lost son, and discovered he has a granddaughter. I can't imagine he wants to leave just as he's getting to know them."

"Yep. I reminded him of that. He said Stella wants him to be with Tony."

"It just doesn't make sense," Betty said. "I can see why you're upset."

"I was stupid to let myself get attached."

"Love is never stupid, Vicki. It just hurts like heck when we lose someone."

I knew Betty understood my feeling of loss. Her husband had died of an aneurism four years ago and she's still grieving.

As is her typical way, Betty suggested some alternatives to consider before I jumped to conclusions. Perhaps Charlie was just expressing his discomfort with the news that Tony was transferred. Maybe he felt safe enough with me to share his feelings.

I wasn't convinced. Regardless of his reasoning, I told Betty, it didn't take away the fact that he's willing to give up his son, his granddaughter, and me.

"That's stretching it a bit, don't you think? When we feel loved and supported, we have the courage to do what we believe we have to do. He's not going to Mars, for God's sake. And he's not giving up anyone."

"Yeah, well I've been down this road before. It's not going to happen again."

"OK, here's what I think," Betty said. "You need time to process everything. Promise me that you'll stop dwelling on the negative. You might want to consider putting the shoe on the other foot."

"How's that?"

"Let's say your company was relocating to St. Louis, and you were asked to move."

"That's not the same and you know it."

"Just bear with me. So, you tell Charlie and he freaks out. What would be your reaction?"

"I don't know."

"Well, think about it," Betty said. "By the way, I made my poustinia reservations for the grand opening weekend at the monastery. What time are you planning to arrive?"

"I don't know if I'm going."

"Of course you're going. Amanda and Sister Tony will be very disappointed if you don't show your support. After all, you concocted the whole scheme of creating a B&B, gift shop, and restaurant, and you orchestrated the donations to make it a reality."

"I don't want to see Charlie."

"Then avoid him. But you have some unfinished business with Charlie. Besides, you're a professional. You know very well how to mask your emotions."

"I'll think about it."

Chapter 8

In the long run, I knew Betty was right. I tried putting myself in Charlie's shoes, but I didn't understand his perspective. Except for Stella. I figured there was still a very strong attachment, despite her death almost forty years ago. It was better to find that out now, rather than later, I thought.

Eventually, my irritation dissipated like morning dew on a sunny day. I recognized that Charlie needed to follow his heart, even if I wasn't included. As Betty noted, his leaving didn't mean that he was abandoning his family or me. Our relationship would just take on a new dimension.

I presumed that Charlie was struggling with my reaction to his dilemma because he hadn't called. Not once. That was a new wrinkle.

Amanda, on the other hand, had called every other night for the past two weeks. Most times, it was a quick request for advice, or just to let me know what she'd been working on to prepare for the grand opening of the B&B and restaurant. She said that Joe and Kate were a big help, especially in the kitchen. She added that Kate planned to be there for the festive weekend, and would double as a waitress, if need be.

I told Amanda that I'd leave work early on Friday, take Harvey over to Myra's house, and arrive in time for the evening meet-and-greet reception. I wanted to beat the rush hour traffic.

"Sounds good," Amanda replied. "Sister Tony suggested that we make hearty appetizers for the weekend guests who'll be coming at various times through the evening. Then we'll offer brunch on Saturday, with dinner service beginning at 4 p.m."

"Why so early?"

"The restaurant's open to the public on Saturday. We think we'll have a crowd."

"Do you have enough staff if you get people from town?"

"GP asked a couple of his buddies from the firehouse to serve with him as waiters and dishwashers. I guess everyone will pitch in."

"I can help if you need me."

"I'll let you know. I think we'll be fine."

It sounded simple, but I knew it wasn't. We agreed that the start-up of the new endeavor will definitely be challenging. I knew it was going to take teamwork to make it successful.

^^^

I called Betty a few nights before my departure to arrange a meet-up time with her. We planned to drop our things off at our poustinias, then head over to the reception together.

"You're sounding a little more chipper," Betty said. "I'm glad you're out of your funk."

"I've done a lot of thinking. I suppose I've come to realize that Charlie's still attached to Stella."

"Could be. Have you talked to him about it?"

"No, he hasn't called."

"You've got a phone."

"I guess I wasn't ready. But I can handle seeing him this weekend, and we may have a chance to have a heart to heart."

"You going to give him an ultimatum?"

"No. Charlie needs to discover what's important to him. If he does go to St. Louis, he'll have the opportunity to reflect on what brought him peace."

"What do you mean?"

"I think it was because of the relationships he forged at the monastery that Charlie's spirit was rekindled. But maybe it was his connection with Tony that brought him contentment. Time will tell."

"That takes a lot of courage on your part."

"It gives me time to decide what I really want. Don't get me wrong. I really like Charlie. I was pretty upset when he said he wanted to follow Tony to St. Louis. But in the long run, I guess I'm not ready to make any kind of commitment."

"That's a good way to look at it. Nothing wrong with just being friends. Speaking of friends, how's Amanda doing with the B&B and restaurant?"

"Sounds like everything's coming together. You know, I never really thought about how difficult it would be to get all of the pieces to fit together. I mean, it's one thing to do renovations to the monastery so the nuns can offer guest rooms for those who don't want solitude in a rustic poustinia, but opening a restaurant's a whole new ball game."

"Yeah, but the nuns need meals anyway," Betty said.

"I know. That's what I was thinking. But it's different with paying guests. You need waiters and dishwashers, people who prep the food, and the line chefs. As it stands, Amanda's counting on volunteers to help get this weekend off the ground. I don't know how she's going to manage through the summer."

"You think she's fizzling out?"

"No, she sounds excited, and Joe's keeping her grounded. I just hope the new nun in charge is supportive. Amanda will be really bummed if everything she's worked for falls apart."

"How about you? It was your brainstorm that started all of this."

"I only planted the seed. Sure, I guess I'll be disappointed if nothing's successful, but it's not my problem."

Betty laughed. "You're a piece of work."

"Why?"

"For starters, you felt a renewed energy when you were trying to save the monastery. You seem mighty disconnected now."

"I wasn't trying to save anything. Just wanted to help the nuns because they were worried about sustaining the place. Besides, now that Sister Tony's been reassigned, I don't see how it's all going to work out."

"Change isn't easy. That's for sure. But who knows? You said this new nun is young. She might have some really cool ideas for how to keep everything afloat."

"Yeah, we'll see."

Chapter 9

S ister Tony greeted Betty and me at the front door when we arrived for the grand opening. We had been chatting about the attractive sign placed at the entrance walkway promoting the *Monastery Restaurant and Inn*. While modest in size, it had distinctive gold lettering, and was a nice fit with the backdrop of the monastery.

"I'm so happy to see you both," Tony said warmly. "I want to introduce you to Sister Marian. She arrived the day before yesterday so that she could be with us this weekend."

"It's nice to meet you," I said, shaking her hand. Betty did the same.

"I've heard so much about both of you from the Sisters, and from Amanda and Joe," Marian said with a charming smile. "I'm looking forward to getting to know you."

I had to admit that the new nun seemed pleasant enough. I'd guess that she was in her mid-30's, and she looked to be fit and trendy. She wore a stylish pant suit, and her long brown hair was pulled back and held with an attractive barrette.

Betty and I poked our heads into the gift shop as Sister Marian led us to the dining room. We said hello to Dolores and Julie, who were both apparently on duty. I could see that Betty was impressed. They had added more inventory since our initial set-up. Betty laughed at the display of hats and visors.

"Let me guess," Betty said to Dolores. "Vicki suggested that you offer visors for the summer patrons."

I explained to Sister Marian that I had purchased a visor at the local drug store last summer after I got sunburned at the lake. Since then, no one had let me live it down.

"I heard about it," Marian chuckled. "Amanda had a fit of laughing when she saw the new items."

I told Sister Dolores that I thought the hat display was a great addition to the gift shop. I was also happy to see that she'd purchased styles that would be appropriate for both men and women.

In fact, Dolores seemed to be enjoying her new role at the monastery. She said that she and Julie would take turns going to the reception in order to keep the gift shop open as the guests arrived. Julie mentioned that the weekend looked like it was going to be profitable. All of the poustinias and rooms in the B&B had been reserved.

"I'll bet you never bargained for all of this when you got assigned here," I said to Sister Marian as we continued down the hallway.

"Actually, I did. The Sisters in our Administration knew it was going to be difficult to find a replacement for Sister Tony. I mean, who wants to run a B&B and restaurant, while also being in charge of a monastery, an infirmary, a gift shop, and a winery? So, they advertised the position in our monthly newsletter and I applied. Lucky for me, I got it."

"It's going to be a lot of work," I said. "And you have big shoes to fill."

Betty nudged me and said, "Yeah, and who's idea was it?"

Sister Marian chuckled, saying, "I heard that Vicki and Charlie cooked up this venture. But I'm excited to be a part of it all. My family owns a farm, and we have apple and strawberry orchards, in addition to the regular barnyard animals. In a way, that's not so different from having a vineyard at the monastery. In fact, I feel right at home already, although I wouldn't mind a few chickens running around."

Two youngish Sisters welcomed us to the dining room. I had never seen them before. Sister Marian introduced them as her two dearest friends, Sister Cheryl and Sister Cathy. She explained that they had come to help her unpack and get settled. They hoped to enjoy some time on the lake when all the hoopla died down.

We were all chatting when Amanda arrived with a tray of Joe's delicious pinwheels. There wasn't an ounce of stress showing in her face.

"I see you've met Marian, Cheryl, and Cathy," Amanda said with a broad smile. "They're the most awesome assistants a chef could want. Not only did they help us get ready for the reception, but they've also prepped everything for tomorrow's brunch."

"It doesn't look like you're going to get much of a break this weekend," I said with a wink to the Sisters. "How long will you be staying?"

"We planned on two weeks," Sister Cathy said, "but we love this place already. We're hoping that Marian and Tony can weave some magic and get us reassigned here. Cheryl teaches grade school, and I teach accounting at a small college in the Midwest. We both have some time off this summer so, if Marian can put up with us, I think we're going to hang around."

"That would be awesome," Amanda said. "Summer's our busiest time here, and I can use all the help I can get."

It pleased me to hear that Amanda was already taking ownership of her role at the *Monastery Restaurant and Inn*. I thought it was great that she'd have some companionship. Even though Marian and her friends are a little older than Amanda, they evidently bring some vitality to the monastery.

^^^

"OK, you guys. It's time to mingle," Amanda announced. "Get yourself some food at the buffet stations. You can have a seat at any of the tables, or you can take a plate to the parlor. Enjoy!"

Betty and I chatted with a few of the guests I hadn't met before, and I noticed Charlie was refilling appetizers in one of the chafing dishes. I excused myself and went to greet him. "Hi, Charlie. How're you doing?"

"Hey, Vicki. Good to see you."

I looked for a sign of nervousness on his part, but I didn't notice anything unusual. I gave him a peck on the cheek, and he grinned.

"We've been so busy around here that I haven't had a chance to call you," he said. "You doing OK?"

"Yeah, I'm good. I just met Sister Marian and her friends. They seem to fit in well around here."

"I like them. That Marian's going to work out fine. She grew up on a farm."

"So I hear. She seems to have a lot of energy."

"Yeah, Tony said she's a fast learner, too. She's been showing her the ropes."

"That'll make for a good transition. I'm glad Marian's also got a couple of friends with her. A move like hers can't be easy."

"They've all been pitching in to get ready for this weekend. Makes me feel not so bad about going to St. Louis."

"So, you're really going?"

"Yeah. You OK about it?"

"I'm fine. You've got to do what you've got to do. We can still keep in touch."

"Definitely. And maybe you can come out there to visit. You ever been to St. Louis?"

"A long time ago. Gateway to the west."

"Yep. That's what they call it."

"And I'm sure you'll be back here for a visit. You've got to keep an eye on your granddaughter."

"Amanda's doing great. I'm really proud of her."

"I am too," I said.

As we were speaking, I noticed that Steve had arrived. He was talking to the new nuns at the entrance of the dining room. I waved him over, figuring that Charlie would probably want to chat with his son. "Steve's here," I said.

"Yeah, he's been coming on weekends to help me move my stuff to the monastery basement. He's going to bunk with me in my poustinia this weekend. We borrowed a cot from the firehouse."

"Hi, Vicki," Steve said when he joined us. "Good to see you again. Hey, Dad. Looks like we've got a crowd coming."

"Gonna be a busy weekend," Charlie said. "You ready to work?"

"Wherever you need me."

I begged off, saying that I wanted to check on the cooking crew. In some ways, I felt like I should be helping, but I didn't want to interfere.

"You guys have some planning to do," I said. "We'll catch up later. I'll put your pan in the kitchen, Charlie."

When I pushed open the kitchen door, I could see that Joe and Kate were busy taking more tasty tidbits out of the oven. Amanda was at the stove, finishing the sauce for the Swedish meatballs.

"You've outdone yourselves." I said. "It smells great in here."

"Hi, Vicki," they replied, seemingly in one voice, barely stopping to look up. "Do we need any refills yet?"

"The cocktail hot dogs are going fast," I said.

"Coming right up," Joe said.

He finished plating a tray and carried it to the dining room. Kate put another pan of hot doggies into the oven.

I turned to Kate, saying, "Your grandmother had a feeling you'd be here this weekend."

"I love this place! Sister Marian said that if we make enough money, she'll hire me for the summer. Wouldn't that be cool?"

"I thought you already have a job lined up."

"I do, but it's only part time during the week. I could do this on weekends."

"I know that Amanda would love to have you working with her. That'd be wonderful."

Amanda agreed wholeheartedly. Joe returned to say they needed more pinwheels. I decided I'd better get out of their way.

When I returned to the dining room, I filled a plate with a variety of hors d'oeuvres. Betty meandered over to me and said that Jeff and Kim had arrived. They were taking their food to the parlor and she'd save me a seat.

I had to admit that I was glad I'd decided to come to the grand opening. I had a good feeling that things would work out fine. A really good feeling.

Chapter 10

Betty and I met at the nun's lake after brunch on Saturday. There was one couple already settled on beach towels at the far side, and another couple out in the canoe. We arranged ourselves in our usual spot. I pulled a wide brimmed straw hat out of my bag.

"You gave up on your visor?" Betty laughed.

"I thought you'd like this better."

"It's nice, but now you're going to have red freckles on your face where the sun peeks through the little holes."

"Give me a break. Who are those people in the canoe?"

"I think their names are Tom and Dianna. They're staying at the B&B. They may be friends of Jeff and Kim Stodges. I didn't get a chance to chat with them too much last night."

"Speaking of Jeff and Kim, do you know what their plans are this afternoon?"

"Kim told me they're going to take a drive into town. Jeff wants to show her the local sights."

"Not much to see," I chuckled. "Just a little farm town."

"Yeah, well, you hot-tailed it there whenever you got stir crazy."

"I never got stir-crazy. Anyway, it's a nice town."

"What did Charlie have to talk about last night?" Betty asked, changing the subject.

"Not much, but he really is going to St. Louis."

"You OK about it?"

"I'm fine, I guess. If you ask me, his plan is short-sighted. The Sisters are going to need him here."

Betty agreed, saying that Charlie knew this place like the back of his hand, probably better than any of the nuns. Surely, she thought, they'd try to convince him to stay.

I told Betty that Charlie's convinced he's making the right decision. In fact, Steve's been helping Charlie move his things to the monastery basement. "And, let me tell you," I added with an emphatic nod, "Charlie's got a lot of stuff in that little cabin."

"If he's not taking it with him, maybe it means he plans to return."

"I doubt it," I said, shaking my head. "Not unless Tony is transferred back. It probably just means he's not intending to build birdhouses in St. Louis."

I watched the couple in the canoe as they approached the platform anchored in the middle of the lake. Charlie was pretty adept at maneuvering the canoe close enough that he could tie it to the side steps of the raft and disembark to fish. The couple must have decided not to try it. They continued on to the other side of the lake.

Betty followed my gaze and giggled at the scene. We both knew that it wasn't easy for two people to synchronize. At least that had been our experience. Our attention was interrupted when we heard our names called. "Hey, Vicki and Betty!"

We glanced up to see Maggie and Ted traipsing across the sand. Betty and I met Maggie last year when she stayed in a poustinia for a week of solitude. She and Ted had been having a rough patch in their marriage, mostly because Maggie couldn't get pregnant. They got things fixed up and, before you knew it, they had a baby boy.

"Well, look what the cat dragged in!" Betty exclaimed. "When did you two arrive?"

"Late last night," Maggie said as she spread her towel on the beach. "Let me introduce you to Ted."

Ted enthusiastically shook our hands, saying how often Maggie spoke about us. It was nice that we'd been able to keep in touch through the year, though Betty was able to get together with Maggie more often than I.

"How's little Dylan?" Betty asked.

"He's doing great, the little stinker. He's the reason we were so late," Maggie said. "My mom's watching him for us this weekend, but he was so fussy that we decided to wait until he settled down before we left."

"You missed a fun party," I said.

"I heard. Actually, your little friend, Amanda, brought us some of the leftovers before they closed up the kitchen. I can't believe she's now a chef, working at the monastery."

"It's amazing," I agreed. "Remember last summer? She was a mess!"

"We liked her friends, too," Maggie said. "We all watched TV in the parlor 'til well after everyone else went to bed. I was afraid we were keeping them up, but they said they needed to unwind."

"That Joe's a nice boy," Ted added. "He sure does have a lot of tattoos."

"Amanda's dad said the same thing when he first met Joe," I said with a chuckle. "But it didn't take him long to see Joe's good qualities."

I explained that Kate's my neighbor's granddaughter. She and Amanda shared an apartment last year. Joe was in the same culinary program, and they all became the best of friends.

"Yeah, we heard," Ted said. "Joe told us about his mentor paying his way through school. Father Jim, I think he said."

"Father Jim's a pretty special guy," I said. "He helped Joe, and now he's working with Joe's mother, who has an alcohol addiction. He was wonderful with Amanda when she lost her baby last year."

"Poor Amanda," Maggie said, with a sad expression in her eyes. "Ted and I had thought of talking to her about adopting her baby before we knew that I was expecting. Betty told us that Amanda had planned to raise her child on her own, so we never approached her."

"It was a difficult time for Amanda, but she weathered it," I said. "Regardless, I'm sure you never get over losing a child. Addison will always be a part of her."

"I can't even imagine," Maggie replied, shaking her head. "I went through a depression when I couldn't conceive. Gosh, if anything ever happened to Dylan, I don't know what I'd do."

"Joe told me that this Father Jim stayed in a cabin for a private retreat a couple of weeks ago," Ted said. "Guess he really liked it because he's come back a few times, just for his day off. In fact, I think he's going to say Mass in the monastery chapel tomorrow. Do you think the nuns would let us attend? I'd like to meet the guy."

"I don't know," I said. "I never got the impression that we were invited to church services. Of course, now that there's a B&B on the premises, maybe they'll open the chapel for guests. Actually, I think I'd like to go, too."

"We could ask Tony tonight," Betty said. "I imagine she'll be at the restaurant for supper. I'm game if the service isn't at the crack of dawn. I planned to sleep in tomorrow."

"You slept in today," I teased.

"Yeah, but I come here to unwind."

"OK, we'll check it out later," Ted said. "I see that the canoe's back on shore. You up for a ride, Maggie?"

"That's what I was hoping. Let's go! Catch you guys later."

^^^

Betty and I watched Maggie and Ted drag the canoe to the water. They teased each other while trying to hold it steady as they embarked. Maggie got the hang of it better than I ever did.

Eventually, I told Betty that I'd had enough sun for the day. She was thinking the same thing, so we began to shake the sand from our towels.

"You going to meet up with Charlie this afternoon?" Betty asked as we trekked up the beach.

"No. He said he's pretty busy today. He's helping to set up the restaurant for tonight, and he's got to train Steve and two of his buddies from the firehouse to help him serve as waiters."

"You're kidding," Betty laughed. "I can't wait to see that!"

"Me either. It should be really interesting."

Jeff and Kim surprised us as we came around the bend in the trees. "What are you two gabbing about?" Jeff asked, flashing his engaging smile.

"Hey, guys. Where've you been?" I countered. "You're missing all of the fun."

"We had plenty of fun ourselves," Jeff replied, looking like the cat that ate the canary. "We took a romantic drive through the countryside." Kim gave him a poke in the ribs.

"You know," Kim said, "I never understood why Jeff liked to come to this place. When he told me about finding a live skunk on his cabin's front porch, I thought he was nuts to pack up his gear every time Sister Tony called to say there was an available cabin. I get it now. There's something special here."

"As Betty would say, 'you've been bitten by the poustinia bug,'" I said. "And now you don't have to rough it in a cabin. Are you enjoying your room at the B&B?"

"It's lovely," Kim said, nodding her agreement. "Amanda did a wonderful job decorating. She sure has a flair for design."

"She got it from her mother," I said. "They'd watch those home remodeling shows on TV together and talk about the blending of texture and harmony. I wouldn't begin to be able to arrange things like she can."

"We had such an enjoyable evening last night. Jeff bought a bottle of wine from the gift shop, and someone even had it chilling in our room for when we went upstairs. Such a nice gesture."

"Sweet," Betty said. "I may have to try the B&B next time I come."

"Not me," I said. "I like the poustinia—especially with the front porch and rocking chair. There's something special about communing with nature."

"You and Jeff can have all the nature you want," Kim chuckled. "Give me the comforts of life. Speaking of comforts, Jeff and I would like the two of you to sit at our table for supper this evening. Did you make your reservations?"

"We had to make reservations for dinner?"

"Yeah. The restaurant's open to the public now."

"Who do I call?" I asked.

"Just use the phone in your cabin," Jeff said. "It's hooked up to the monastery. Sister Julie's going to be in charge of all reservations now that Tony's leaving. I'm pretty sure they're counting that all of us who are staying the weekend will be at the restaurant tonight. Just call to confirm. Our reservations are for 6 p.m."

Betty and I promised to make arrangements as soon as we got back to our respective cabins. I was looking forward to a pleasant evening with my monastery friends.

Chapter 11

I thought the outfit that I'd brought to wear at the restaurant was perfect for the festive occasion. In fact, I knew that Amanda would be pleased with my selection. She'd spent much of the past year trying to remodel me and my wardrobe. It's not easy to teach an old dog new tricks.

Balloons were tied to the *Monastery Restaurant and Inn* sign at the front walkway, and I noticed that the parking lot was full. I actually had butterflies in the pit of my stomach. Guess I'm not as disconnected as Betty thought. I really wanted everything to go well.

Betty and I had walked to the monastery together, both surprised when Sister Julie greeted us at the front door. She invited us to browse the gift shop or sit in the parlor until our number was called. She even handed me one of those little buzzer thingies that would announce when our table was ready.

We found Jeff and Kim Stodges in the parlor, chatting with a few of the other B&B guests. Jeff introduced us to the couple we'd seen at the lake earlier and we chatted about the intricacies of balancing a canoe. Jeff teased us, reminding us of the health benefits of paddling. He was the one who had donated the canoe, so I knew there was no use arguing the point.

Jeff, Kim, Betty, and I didn't have too long a wait before our buzzers signaled an available table. Charlie met us at the doorway of the dining room and ushered us to our location. He looked quite dapper in black trousers and a powder-blue golf shirt with the *Monastery Restaurant and Inn* logo embroidered over the breast pocket. In fact, I noticed that each of the waiters was wearing the same uniform as Charlie. It certainly added a classy touch.

The dining room was totally full. Sister Marian was at the cash register checking out several patrons, and one of Charlie's buddies was bussing tables. I waved to the group of Sisters who were seated at two tables by the window and said hi to the guests I recognized as we passed by.

We had barely checked out the full-page menu after we took our seats when Amanda's dad, Steve, arrived to fill our water glasses. He told us that he'd be our waiter for the evening.

"I like the outfit, Steve," I said with an affirming smile. "It makes you look experienced."

"My students should see me now. They'd be rolling in the aisles laughing."

"They'd probably be impressed, knowing their professor at the university could let down his hair, so to speak."

"Yeah. Right." Steve stifled a chuckle before telling us that he'd be back in a few moments to take our orders.

It didn't take me long to decide that I was having the rib eye steak smothered in onions and mushrooms. I chose a twice-baked potato and green beans with toasted almonds for my sides. Jeff ordered the same, while Kim and Betty each selected the broiled salmon with couscous and a side of coleslaw. Jeff also ordered two bottles of wine for our table.

Steve returned in no time with the pinot noir, one of the nuns' most popular wine made from their grapes. It reminded me of some of my best memories of the place last year when I helped with the harvest. Steve popped the corks and gave each of us a generous portion.

"Can you join us, Steve?" Kim asked.

"Believe me, I wish I could. Maybe later, OK?"

"Any time you need a rest, just pull a chair over."

"Sounds good. I'll be back soon with your food."

I felt guilty that I wasn't helping but shrugged it off when Jeff raised his wine glass and proposed a toast. "Congratulations to the nuns for having the courage to open their home and their hearts to each of us, and to Vicki for planting the seed. Cheers!"

I giggled, saying, "They're probably ready to kill me."

"Look around," Jeff said. "Tony has a grin on her face to the like I've never seen. Charlie's about ready to bust a seam. Isn't that the Holtz family over there in the corner? They look like they're having a good time."

We had all helped the Holtz's with apple picking at their orchard last fall. Another happy memory. I waved across the room to them, and they waved back. Sister Dolores was chatting with them but stopped by our table on her way out.

"I have to get back to the gift shop, but I hope you're going to try the seafood combo. The garlic sauce is to die for!"

"Are you exhausted yet?" I asked.

"Not a bit. Well, maybe a little. We've been crazy busy selling merchandise in the store. Cheryl and Cathy relieved me, so I could eat, and now they'll relieve Julie with the reservations. Things should start to slow down soon."

"What's the big seller?"

"The wine, definitely. Charlie's going to have to bring up more cartons from the basement. And darn if Julie's jellies aren't flying off the shelves. Don't get me wrong. Her jelly's great, but everyone loves those stupid little bows and labels decorating the jars."

"Don't close up shop before we leave," Kim said. "I want to get some of them to take as gifts for my friends."

"Julie will be thrilled, but I get sick and tired of watching her spend so much time making the jars pretty. Good thing she prepared plenty of batches after our big grape harvest last year, though. Now she says she's going to buy strawberries to make jam when these run out."

"That's great," I said. "You should have a good return from this weekend."

"Without a doubt. I'd better get back or Julie's going to have a fit that she hasn't eaten yet. Stop by on your way out."

Dolores scurried off as Steve arrived with four steaming plates of food. As he served, I asked, "How's the cooking crew holding up?"

"They're starting to look a little frazzled, but they're OK. It's been non-stop since we opened. Amanda's getting worried that, despite all of her planning, they may run out of some menu items."

"That's probably not so bad," I said. "I mean, after all, they didn't know exactly how many people would arrive."

"Yeah, lots of people didn't make reservations until the last minute." Betty kicked me under the table.

"I'm guilty," I said.

"You were counted in because you booked a weekend here. I'm talking about all the folks from town who showed up. We were kind of surprised. Even Jake from the diner is here with his wife. In fact, once in a while he pops into the kitchen to give the kids a pep talk. It's kind of cool."

"That's really amazing. Joe told me that Jake's been really helpful. Gives him advice, and even shares recipes."

"Jake's a nice guy, for sure. Can I get you anything else before I check on my other tables?"

"Nah, we're good," Jeff said, reaching for the pepper. I had already scooped a forkful of the potato topping but nodded my agreement.

^^^

While we were eating our meal and chatting about all of the recent changes at the monastery, I followed Charlie with my eyes. As when he oversaw the grape harvests, he orchestrated all of the up-front and behind-the-scene activities, making for an organized opening night of the restaurant.

He quietly directed the wait staff, brought guests to their tables, and even helped serve. I chuckled to myself when I heard him tell Steve that he hoped they didn't run out of cherry pie before he got a piece.

Betty followed my gaze. "That's so funny," she said with a grin. "Charlie does like his pie."

"Speaking of Charlie," Jeff said as he put a piece of steak on his fork, "he told me he's going to St. Louis with Tony. This place will be different without the two of them."

"It will be," Betty agreed, "but change can be good."

"Yeah, I like Tony's new replacement," Jeff said. "We had a conversation with her last night. She seems to be grounded in the mission of this place. Don't get me wrong. Once she settles in, I think she's going to add her own vision. She's smart, though. I don't think she'll make many changes until she gets the lay of the land."

"I'd also like to see her friends involved," I added. "They both bring some strengths that could benefit the monastery. They were talking about possibly being reassigned here."

"That's probably a good idea," Jeff said. "I know Tony was running out of steam trying to keep this place afloat. Dolores and Julie have been a good support to her, but they're not spring chickens any more. I'm glad they're going to run the gift shop and take over the reservations side of the enterprise. Those activities won't be too strenuous on them, but it'll show a strong presence of the nuns to the public."

"You think that's important?" Betty asked.

"Yeah, I do. One of the reasons I've liked coming to the monastery is because of the spirit of the Sisters. I don't mean in a spiritual way, although that's probably a part of it. Tony and the girls never pushed religion on their guests. But they showed us that tranquility enables us to think beyond ourselves. To see ourselves in the context of a bigger picture."

Jeff gave all of us something to think about. I could see why he'd risen to the top of the corporate ladder. He's grounded and principled and uses solitude to fuel his wisdom and insight.

Steve came by to take our orders for dessert, telling us the options. Kim, Betty, and I ordered the chocolate mousse, and Jeff got coconut custard pie. "I sure don't want to take the last piece of cherry pie," Jeff said with a wink. "Tell your dad I saved it for him."

"He'll be mighty grateful."

We were all laughing when we noticed that the Sisters had finished and were leaving the dining room. Tony stopped to chat as she passed by. She told us she wasn't sure she'd see us before we departed, and she wanted to thank us for our support of the Sisters' endeavors.

Jeff stood to give her a kiss on the cheek. "We're really going to miss you, Tony. Kim and I wish you much success in your new mission."

Sister Tony responded with a simple thank you. I knew this was difficult for her. Before she joined the other Sisters, I asked if church services might be open to the guests.

"Definitely. We have Mass at 9:30 a.m. Actually, Father Jim will be joining us tomorrow, and he's staying for breakfast. You'd be most welcome. In fact, I'll get the word around to those who may be interested. Entrance is through the side door of the chapel."

By the time we finished dessert and paid for our meals, we noticed only a few stragglers coming into the restaurant. Cheryl and Cathy were among them. They looked tired.

"Busy evening for the two of you," Jeff said. "Hope they have some food left."

"We do, too," Cheryl chuckled. "But, if not, it's OK. We'll munch on leftovers as we help the chefs clean up."

"I hope they didn't close the gift shop yet," Kim said.

"Not yet, but soon. Dolores and Julie are pooped."

"I'm sure they are," I said, nodding my head. "They'll be happy to call it a night."

Betty and I said good night to Jeff and Kim at the entrance to the gift shop. We decided to take a stroll along the main drive before returning to our cabins. I reminded her that it was just about a year ago that we met on my first visit to the monastery. She had told me all about the place, even showed me the shortcut to the lake. We both agreed that we knew right away we'd be friends.

"You glad you came this weekend?" Betty asked.

"Oh, yeah. It's been amazing."

"You made it all happen."

"I was only a small cog in the wheel. The Sisters made it all happen. I'm just happy to have been a part of it."

We stopped to rest at the fallen tree by the creek, just beyond the vineyard. The setting sun gleamed its rays through the barely rustling leaves to produce colorful sparkles on the surface of the water. I found this spot to be particularly restful, reinforcing the serenity I experienced whenever I returned to the poustinias. I knew Betty felt the same sentiment.

"We should plan another visit soon," Betty said. "How about a week at the end of July"

"Sounds good to me. I want a cabin, though, not the B&B."

"Me, too."

Reluctant to leave our peaceful location, but recognizing that darkness was approaching, we began our trek back to our cabins. I asked Betty if she planned to attend church services in the morning.

"No, I decided I'd better head home. I have to prep for a couple of court cases. You going?"

"Yeah. I want some time with Amanda and Charlie before leaving. Guess I just need to make sure they're both OK."

"They're fine," Betty said. "But I'm glad you're back in the game."

"What game?"

"You know. Life."

"Yeah, I know. I'll call you during the week."

"Good. I want to hear about your conversation with Charlie."

"I told you I'm OK with his leaving. I just want to wish him well."

"Yeah. Right," Betty said with a grin as she continued on the path to her cabin.

I sat on my porch, watching the fireflies and reflecting on the contentment I'd felt since coming here. My world seemed so much larger, especially with this new circle of friends. I knew in my heart that I was lucky they were a part of my life. I've been enriched in ways I'd never expected.

Chapter 12

I met Maggie and Ted at the side entrance of the chapel on Sunday morning. I don't think I'd have had the courage to go in without them. It's been a long time since I've attended a church service.

The chapel is the entire footprint of the east wing of the monastery. Beautiful stained-glass windows surround the main floor, with a second-level balcony where the infirmary Sisters can participate from their wheel chairs. I could envision that, at one time, the entire chapel had been filled with young women beginning their training as novices and postulants. Now only the first two pews in front of the altar were occupied with Sisters.

I followed Maggie and Ted into the row behind Charlie, Steve, Amanda, Joe, and Kate. Charlie turned slightly to wink his approval of my arrival. I had a feeling he was a regular attendee. Before long, Father Jim emerged in priestly attire, and one of the older Sisters began playing the organ.

I wasn't quite sure when to kneel or stand, but Maggie whispered that I should just follow her lead. She also handed me a prayer booklet to follow for the readings and responses. I was a little overwhelmed with everything until Father Jim began to preach.

I was completely mesmerized by Father Jim's sermon. It was nothing like I had ever experienced. No fire and brimstone.

No boring lecture. I felt as if he was talking directly to me, just from the heart. Kind of lifting me up and challenging me to be more authentic, more thoughtful, and more kind. I wondered if the others got the same message.

The final hymn was one I remembered from my youth. Once Maggie showed me the place in the hymnal, I sang with the rest of the congregation. It was energizing, as if a part of my soul was awakening.

After the service, Maggie and Ted said they were going to do some last-minute packing but would see me at the brunch. Charlie gave me a quick peck on the cheek before he and Steve scurried off to catch up with Joe to prepare for the arrival of the guests.

I joined Amanda and Kate on a more leisurely walk to the dining room. Both were in good spirits, despite their early prep work in the kitchen. They said everything was ready for Sunday brunch and the crew was hoping for another good turnout.

"Aren't you tired?" I asked.

"No more than our final weeks in culinary school," Kate said with a grin. "We got good training, that's for sure."

"Well, you did an amazing job this weekend. The meals were delicious, and the accommodations were superb."

"Thanks," Amanda said, looking as proud as a peacock. "Aunt Tony and the nuns are happy about everything. Things went pretty well 'til we ran out of food."

"Did you have to send people away?"

"No. We just removed the menus and offered specials of things we still had. It all worked out, thanks to Joe and Kate."

"I'm proud of each of you. Still, the responsibility was on your shoulders, Amanda. You forged ahead even when things were difficult. That's what a real leader does."

Kate gave Amanda a high-five, while Amanda assured me that it was a team effort. Even the Sisters assisted with food prep and clean-up, she added. Cheryl and Cathy had been the most helpful, and they promised to meet the crew at the lake after all of the guests departed.

"They're really cool," Kate said. "Amanda and I hope they can stay here."

"Me, too. When are GP and Tony going to St. Louis?"

"They're leaving Friday," Amanda said. "Sister Marian's planning a farewell party for them on Thursday night. I'm calling it the 'Last Supper,' and I'm going to wrap up that picture from the dining room for Aunt Tony."

"You think she's going to want to take it with her?"

"Probably not, but I think it'll make her laugh. At least I'll get rid of it."

"You OK about your grandfather going with her?"

"Yeah, I'm cool. It's not like I'm that attached or anything. How are you feeling about it? I mean, he's kind of like leaving you behind."

"I have to admit, I was a little upset when he first told me about it. But, I'm fine. And, you never know. He may come back."

"Between you and me," Amanda whispered as we neared the dining room, "I don't think Aunt Tony's too crazy about the idea. But, whatever."

^^^

I had forgotten that the brunch was planned for the guests and nuns this morning, not open to the public. No wonder Kate and Amanda had been in no hurry. They went to sit with Father Jim and Joe. Charlie waved for me to join him, Marian, and Tony. We pulled up an extra chair for Steve. The rest of the Sisters and guests mixed and mingled.

After Sister Tony said the blessing, Joe brought a large pan of sausage and egg casserole from the kitchen and placed it on the table next to a tray of coffee cake and pastries. Coffee, tea, and juice were also available. Amanda announced that we were all invited to serve ourselves.

"It was a wonderful weekend," I said to those at my table. "You must be relieved that everything went so well."

"Thanks be to God!" Tony said with a sigh. "Seriously," she continued, "even though Amanda was upset that they ran out of a few menu items, the entire event was a great success. I have to admit, though, in many ways I'm happy to pass the baton to Marian."

"I wish I had a little more time to work with you, Tony, before I'm on my own," Marian said. "This weekend was rather chaotic."

"You'll be fine," Tony replied. "In fact, now you'll be able to put your own spin on things. This place needs new blood. The biggest challenge will be to keep everything in perspective. The poustinias, the vineyards, the restaurant, the B&B, and the gift shop are here to provide the resources we need to sustain the community. Don't let them run your life or sap the spirit of the monastery. Channel them so they bring others to solitude and tranquility."

"Easier said than done," Marian said, shaking her head.

"Without a doubt," Tony agreed. "That's why I'm happy that you're now in charge." We all laughed.

Charlie and Steve were the first to return after heaping their plates with every buffet item. I had to admit that the egg and sausage duo looked good. So did the two of them. They're so much alike, at least in personality. Charlie said Steve took after his mother, but I can see Charlie in him as well.

"Did you both stay up half the night packing Charlie's stuff?" I asked as I stood to take my turn at the buffet table.

"Are you kidding?" Steve asked with a wry grin. "I was so pooped last night, I was asleep before my head hit the pillow."

"Well, you snored like a truck driver. Kept me awake half the night."

"Speak for yourself, Pop. You were sawing wood before I even made it to the cot."

"Regardless," I interjected, "you both outdid yourselves last night. Hope you can take some time to unwind today."

"Lugging boxes," Steve replied with a chuckle. "I might stay another day or two. I'm going to miss this guy."

"Me, too," I added as I took my plate to the buffet line.

I noticed that my comment brought a sadness to Charlie's eyes. It made me think of Robert Frost's poem about the road not taken. Both directions held promise, but only one could be followed. Choosing the right way was one of life's most difficult challenges, I thought.

When everyone finished eating, Father Jim suggested that we move our chairs into a large circle. Maggie and Ted and a few of the guests said they had to leave, but the rest of us were able to join the fun. It was too bad that Betty missed this part of the weekend. She'd have enjoyed it.

Jeff shared a few hilarious tales of his cabin experiences and Father Jim added some of his own. Most centered on the critters they encountered in the woods. Regardless, it was a time of camaraderie and bantering, cementing the unity that we all felt was a culmination of this weekend.

Chapter 13

Eventually, I saw Amanda giving Joe a nod that she wanted to start the clean-up. I knew the young folks planned to go to the lake, and it was a glorious day to enjoy the sunny afternoon. Since Charlie had offered to help me bring my things from the poustinia to my car, I signaled to him that I was ready to leave. While he went to get the golf cart, I began saying my farewells to the group.

"Hope to see you both again soon," I said to Jeff and Kim. "Will you be returning to the B&B this summer?"

"No doubt about it," Kim replied with a grin. "I think Jeff has already booked our next weekend."

"Betty and I made cabin reservations for next month. We still like rustic."

"Me, too," Jeff countered. "But I like having my better half with me, so B&B it is."

"Smart man," Father Jim noted, on his way to the kitchen with a few empty trays. We all had a good laugh.

I offered to help, but everyone reminded me that Charlie was waiting. Part of me knew that it was time to go, but I was dreading the inevitable good-bye with Charlie. Sister Tony may have sensed my reluctance. She hooked her arm in mine, and we walked together to the front entrance.

"I'm sorry that Charlie decided to go to St. Louis," she said. "I know that must have been upsetting to you."

"I was surprised. I guess I just realized that he's still very attached to Stella. And you represent Stella in his mind. It's better to find that out now, rather than later."

"That's an interesting way of looking at it. Honestly, I can't figure out why this is so important to him. I think he's going to be needed here."

"I do, too. What's he going to do in St. Louis? Are the nuns going to support him?"

"No. I already told him he's going to have to get a job. He found a room at a boarding house near the convent where I'll be staying, and he may be able to work as a custodian at one of our schools. Still, I don't think he realizes that things are going to be different."

"He might return here when he comes to his senses."

"Don't give up on him," Tony said. "I think the two of you are good for each other."

"I guess time will tell. In the meantime, I hope you'll stay in touch."

"Definitely," Tony said as she gave me a hug.

∧∧∧

Charlie was waiting for me at the front entrance. As much as I had wanted to have some time alone with Charlie, I was feeling apprehensive. I hoped I wouldn't break down in tears, or act like the proverbial jilted woman.

"Your carriage awaits," Charlie said with a gallant wave of his arm. Then he took my hand to help me into the golf cart. When he maneuvered onto the driveway, I reminded him how much he's going to miss this place. He nodded his agreement.

"You sure you really want to go?" I asked.

"Yeah."

"This was a nice weekend," I said. "It's just about a year since my first visit here."

"I know. I was thinking that."

"Betty and I made poustinia reservations for a week at the end of July."

"That'll be good."

"I want to help with the grape harvest again this fall. You going to come back to be in charge of it?"

"I don't know. Probably not. I figure I'll have a job or something."

"Guess you can't just pick up to go harvest the grapes."

"Don't think so."

"Who do you think could take over the harvest?"

"I don't know. Marian might have to do it. Anyway, she grew up on a farm. She knows about bringing in a crop."

"That's true," I said as we reached my poustinia. "I'll get my things and be right out."

"You need any help?"

"No, I was able to fit everything in my suitcase. Give me a minute to freshen up."

When I returned, Charlie said, "I'm going to miss you." He had turned the golf cart around and was waiting at the rear of the cart. He lifted my bag into the back.

"I'm going to miss you, too."

Once again, Charlie made sure I safely slid into the front seat before getting behind the wheel. He slowly drove to my car in the parking lot. Finally, he said, "You know, I wasn't leading you on. I really have feelings for you."

"I know, Charlie. I have feelings for you, too."

"We said we'd take it slow," he said. I laughed out loud.

"What's that mean?" he asked, with a hurt expression on his face.

"I'm sorry. That just struck me as funny. Yes, we said we'd take it slowly."

"You sure you're not mad at me?"

"I was. But I'm not anymore," I said as we pulled up to my car. "I think of you as a good friend, Charlie. I'm happy that I had a chance to get to know you and work with you. We made a good team."

Charlie seemed to mull over my words as he carried my bag to the car. "It was kind of more than just a good team," he said. "I might be back."

"You think you might?"

"Maybe. Just depends. You going to wait for me?"

"For what?"

"Well, like maybe to see what the future holds."

"I'm going to live for today, Charlie; not the future. And today I know that you're my friend, and I wish you the best as you travel to St. Louis."

I gave him a hug. He hugged me back, then kissed my cheek. As I settled into the car, I said, "Now, you take care of Tony. This move isn't easy for her. She's going to need you."

"Yeah, I will," he said as I pulled out of the driveway.

Chapter 14

The next four weeks whizzed by. I needed to tie up loose ends at work in order to arrange my coming vacation. That usually had me staying late or working through the weekend. Myra agreed to watch Harvey during the time I'd be away. I didn't know what I'd do without her.

Amanda and I chatted on the phone at least once a week, and she often texted me when a new development had occurred at the monastery. She told me that things had settled down since the grand opening of the B&B and restaurant. She was feeling good about managing the daily operations.

Myra and I were talking on her front porch one evening before my departure. I had stopped over when I got home from work, so I could confirm the arrangements about Harvey. Funny thing was, Myra used to tease me about staying alone in a cabin in the woods. Now she seemed to like encouraging me to go to the poustinia.

"Are you ready for your week at that monastery?" she asked as we watched a particularly active butterfly flit through her garden.

"Just about all set," I said. "I need to do some laundry and pack my bag. I'll stop at the store after work tomorrow to get the groceries I'll need to take with me."

"I suppose now that they have the restaurant there, you don't need to bring as much food to prepare in the cabin."

"That's true, but I'm not sure how often I'll dine at the monastery. I'm in new territory there. Guess I'll get enough to tide me over, then play it by ear."

"That makes sense. Any news from Amanda?"

"She said that the two young Sisters who helped the new nun get settled received word that they'll be staying. They've been assigned to live at the monastery."

"That's wonderful. Kate said that she likes them. She told me they've really helpful in the kitchen."

"I noticed that as well. You know, they're not that much older than Amanda and Kate, and they're really down to earth. You happy that Kate was offered the weekend chef position?"

"Sure. I think it's a good experience for her, and she likes working with Amanda. She told me that Amanda rearranged her own room with two twin beds, so Kate wouldn't need a guest room. They probably stay up half the night talking when Kate arrives."

"Either that, or they drive each other crazy. You know Amanda can sometimes be a little testy."

"Kate can handle it," Myra said with a chuckle. "Do they get a lot of guests at the B&B?"

"Sounds like it's more popular on weekends."

I told Myra that the poustinias tended to draw those who wanted a private retreat, usually on a weekly basis. That made it easier on the cooking crew since the guests who preferred to rough it brought their own groceries.

"But you could eat at the restaurant if you wanted to?" Myra asked. "Even if you're staying in a cabin?"

"That was the plan. I'm just not sure about the process. I mean, maybe you need a reservation."

"Is it that complicated?"

"It is when you factor in how many meals are needed for each service and how much food to purchase. Amanda's got to make trays for the Sisters in the infirmary, meals for the other nuns, and figure out which of the guests will also be eating. Plus, the restaurant's open to the public on weekends."

Myra shook her head, her expression one of disbelief. "And this was your idea? Poor Amanda. No wonder she's happy that Kate was hired to help with the cooking."

I reminded Myra that Joe also volunteered his time in the evenings and on weekends. The Sisters probably recognized the overwhelming task and assigned Cheryl and Cathy to assist. In the end, once all the kinks are worked out, the enterprise could provide a sizable revenue source for the nuns.

I could see that Myra's interest was piqued. She indicated that she'd like to see the place, maybe even offer her services in the kitchen. I told her that I thought she should book a weekend. I felt certain she'd enjoy a getaway.

"I don't know. Quite honestly, I'd rather be there when you're staying, but we can't do that if I'm watching Harvey."

"That's true. I wonder if Sister Marian would ever let me bring the mutt. I've always said he'd love exploring the woods."

Myra suggested that I check it out. She said she'd prefer to stay in the comfort of the B&B. With her arthritis, she couldn't do a lot of walking.

I reminded her that they have a golf cart. Someone would drive her wherever she wants to go. I added, "I'm not sure who'll be doing the driving, now that Tony and Charlie have left."

"You told me about Sister Tony. Why didn't you mention Charlie?"

"I don't know. Guess it wasn't important."

"Seems pretty monumental to me. I thought you two were becoming a couple. Come to think about it, you don't talk about him anymore."

"There's nothing to talk about. Charlie's gone."

"Don't bury your feelings."

"I'm not burying anything, Myra. Let it go."

I didn't mean to snap at Myra, but I was tired of everyone feeling sorry for me. For heaven's sake, it wasn't like Charlie or I had made a commitment. Neither of us was ready, and that's the fact of the matter.

In a more gentle tone, I asked if she needed anything at the grocery store. Myra said she'd already done her shopping for the week, but she'd give me a call if she thought of anything. "Just get plenty of treats for me to give Harvey. What time are you leaving on Saturday?"

"I'll bring him over about 10 a.m., if that's OK with you. That'll get me to the monastery by noon. I'm meeting Betty for lunch, just after I check in."

"Sounds like a plan," Myra said. "I'll see you then."

Chapter 15

B etty and I had timed our arrival at the monastery pretty well. She pulled into the parking lot only minutes before I did, and she was waiting for me by her car. We walked together to the gift shop to pay for our reservations.

Sister Julie welcomed us with her charming smile. "It's good to see you both. What a great week for your stay with us. I heard the weather's supposed to be lovely."

"I'm so ready for some peace and quiet," I said. "You don't know how much I've been looking forward to this getaway."

"Me, too," Betty added with a wry grin. "Why is it that all hell breaks loose whenever you try to get ready for a vacation?"

Julie processed our credit cards, and said she'd take us to our cabins when Dolores returned from lunch. She suggested that we might want to get lunch in the restaurant while we were waiting.

"That was our plan," Betty said, nodding her agreement. "How's everything going with the gift shop?"

"We've settled into a nice rhythm. Dolores is much less stressed now that we've launched regular hours of operation."

Julie explained that the gift shop remained open for three hours each morning during the week. On weekends, she and Dolores took shifts, so they could offer extended hours. "We also now have a better idea of what people might want to purchase. We don't want to overstock inventory that isn't necessary."

"The two of you make a good team," I said. "You really complement one another."

"If anything, we drive each other crazy," Julie chuckled. "But that's why we're friends. Now go get something to eat, and I'll meet you back here when you're ready."

A couple of the nuns and three guests were in the dining room when we arrived. Kate greeted us at the door and told us to sit wherever we preferred. When Amanda told me that Kate was hired for the weekends, I had thought they'd be working in the kitchen together. Guess I hadn't considered that a restaurant also needed hospitality and wait staff.

Betty and I stopped to talk with the Sisters at their table. I told them how happy I was to hear that Cheryl and Cathy were now permanent fixtures. Marian was the first to reply. "You and me both. I don't know how I'd manage without them."

"At least we keep you laughing," Cathy countered.

"No doubt about it. Especially when you managed to get yourselves skunked two weeks ago."

"Yeah. That was Cheryl's fault. I thought I'd never get the smell off me."

Cheryl piped up. "We'll be a little more careful next time we check to see that the cabins are ready for guests."

Betty and I were still giggling when we seated ourselves at a table by the entry kiosk. As I gazed around the dining room, I noticed that several attractive pictures of grape vines had been strategically placed on the walls. A live ficus tree was arranged near the window in the far corner, and a few other potted plants enhanced the décor.

Kate brought us glasses of ice water and gave us a menu. It didn't take us long to both decide on the turkey sandwich with lettuce and tomatoes. After she placed our order, I invited Kate to join us.

"I guess I can sit for a few minutes," Kate said, "but I have to keep an eye on my tables. Amanda's going to be out to see you shortly."

"How's everything going?" Betty asked.

"Pretty good. Do you like the new decor? Sister Marian thought we should highlight the vineyards. It's kind of like our trademark."

"Lovely," I said as Amanda arrived with our sandwiches.

"What's lovely?" she asked, giving me a hug.

"The new art work. I hear you're focusing on a grape and harvest theme."

"Yeah. I think it's cool. Definitely better than what we had before. Sister Marian and I went to an art gallery at the outlet mall, and she let me choose the prints that fit my design."

"She probably noticed that you have a flair for color and balance."

"Maybe. But I think she's just letting me do my job. She's good about that. Like she doesn't interfere but has some classy ideas. She did give me another responsibility."

"How can you handle anything else?" Betty asked.

"I'm excited about it. It's really neat. I'll show you when you finish eating."

Kate and Amanda excused themselves when two newly-arriving guests stood waiting at the entrance. Kate greeted them and led them to a table. As she departed, Amanda suggested that Betty and I come to the kitchen after lunch. She wanted to see our reaction to the new addition.

The Sisters stopped by our table as they were leaving. Cathy and Cheryl mentioned that they were heading to the lake for an hour of relaxation.

"We'll be there, too," Betty said. "We just have to drop off our things at the cabins. We're also going to see about Amanda's surprise, whatever that is."

"You talking about Amanda's additional duties?" Marian asked. I noticed that the Sisters were grinning.

"Yeah, she said something about a new job," I said.

"Definitely a new task," Cathy said with a giggle.

"What is it?"

"You'll have to see for yourself. Suffice it to say, Amanda will be busy."

"Seems like she's already got her hands full."

That sent the nuns into fits of laughter. "Yep," Cathy said. "Her hands are definitely going to be full. You can tell us what you think when you get to the lake. See you later!"

^^^

Betty and I entered the kitchen just as Amanda finished plating the new orders. Amanda led us through the pantry and out the back door. There in the yard was a new fenced area and a fairly large coop. Six chickens and a rooster were pecking the ground.

"Oh, my gosh! You have chickens!" I exclaimed.

"It's my job to feed them and collect the eggs every day," Amanda said proudly. "Isn't that cool?"

"I never thought I'd see the day when you'd be excited to take care of real live chickens."

"I think it's awesome. The hens lay eggs every 25 hours, so pretty much I'll collect six eggs every morning. Marian got a rooster, so we'll have some baby chicks. The birds and bees kind of stuff. You know what I mean?"

"So much for sleeping late around here," Betty moaned. "The rooster will probably have us up at the crack of dawn."

"Yeah, he's an early bird," Amanda said with a wink. "Get it? Early bird?"

"Got it. Where'd you get the coop?"

"Sister Marian ordered it on-line, and Joe put it together. It's nice and sturdy."

"I guess Marian wasn't kidding when she mentioned she wanted chickens," I said. "Next thing you know, you'll be feeding goats in the field."

"How'd you know she wants to get a couple of goats?"

"I was only teasing."

"Yeah, well she does. But they'll feed themselves in the field. She doesn't want to have to cut the grass. She grew up on a farm."

"So I've heard."

"You going to have to milk the goats?" Betty asked.

"You're being silly. Well, actually, Kate says it would be kind of neat to make goat cheese."

"Are you OK with all of this?" I asked. "Seems a bit more than you bargained for."

"It's all cool. We have weekly planning meetings for the B&B, restaurant, and gift shop. I'm invited to attend and share my ideas."

Amanda seemed to be thriving in this new environment. She doesn't do well when she's ignored or made to feel that her thoughts are insignificant. Sister Marian apparently has a talent for recognizing the strengths of others. I was hoping I'd have an opportunity this week to get to get to know her better.

"It sounds like you really like Marian."

"Yeah, she's great. I really like Cathy and Cheryl, too."

"You're not missing your aunt?"

"Aunt Tony's great, too. Just in a different way. Like I was really upset when she was transferred, but it's all working out. You know what I mean?"

"I feel the same way," I said. "I resisted the change, but I love the playfulness that's unfolding before my eyes."

"Joyful encounters," Betty said.

"What do you mean?" Amanda asked.

"It just seems like the new Sisters are sharing their joy at being assigned to the monastery. Their exuberance is rubbing off on everyone they meet."

"That's true," Amanda said. "It's really neat to be a part of this place. Not that I want to be a nun or anything."

"I didn't think so," I said with a chuckle.

Chapter 16

Sister Cathy waved to Betty and me as we approached the lake. I noticed that one of the guests was fishing from the anchored raft, and it reminded me of Charlie. He used to spend many of his summer mornings on the platform, catching enough catfish to provide a nice supper for the nuns.

Betty and I spread our towels next to Cathy and Cheryl, settling ourselves on the sandy beach. I made sure to put on my hat and lather on the suntan lotion. I learned the hard way last summer that I tended to burn on my first days in the sun.

"You two been swimming?" Betty asked.

"We didn't plan on it," Cheryl said with a comical smirk. "Cathy lost her footing when we got into the canoe. Darn if that water isn't cold."

"It never really warms up, but it's more manageable by the end of August," I said, thinking about my own experience last summer. "Unless you're really brave."

Cathy and Cheryl both giggled, assuring me that taking a swim in an ice bath wasn't on their bucket list. Instead, they'd just enjoy the beauty of the nature.

"Speaking of nature, how'd you like our chickens?" Cathy asked.

"The chickens are fine," Betty replied. "But the rooster's got to go."

"Awww. He's a fine boy. Think of it this way. You won't need an alarm clock."

"Yeah, well you probably all get up at the crack of dawn anyway," Betty said. "I'm here for the peace and quiet."

"You won't even hear him from your cabin," Cheryl said. "I promise."

Betty didn't look very convinced. I was a little skeptical myself, more because I didn't think Amanda needed one more task to oversee. Still, I knew Amanda well enough. She'd have a fit if she wasn't happy about something.

"Sister Tony said you've been coming to the monastery poustinias for several years," Cathy remarked to Betty, changing the subject. "How'd you discover this place?"

"I guess I was one of the first guests," Betty replied. "I was looking for a rental cabin with a lake. I wanted some solitude to unwind, and this place fit the bill. Besides, it reminded me of a camp that my husband and I used to frequent."

I explained that Betty's an attorney, and she works with poor or disadvantaged families in the city. Before her husband died, they'd often bring kids for a weekend at the camp.

"That's wonderful," Cheryl said. "What about you, Vicki?"

"I found a brochure at my post office. I thought the place might help me figure out what to do in my retirement. Instead I found four new friends."

"What do you do?"

"I'm VP of Human Resources at a publishing firm. Been there 39 years. Amanda thinks I should stay. She lived with me last summer and had a temp job there."

"She told us. Said you helped her get through a difficult time."

"I think we were good for each other. I wouldn't have even considered sharing my space until Betty told me what she and her husband, John, did to help teens. Having Amanda stay with me was a life-changing experience."

"So, are you going to retire?" Cheryl asked.

"Not yet. I haven't figured out what I'd enjoy doing with my spare time. What made you decide that you wanted to be assigned to the monastery?"

"I guess I saw the massive responsibilities that Marian was facing," Cheryl said. "Don't get me wrong. She's extremely capable and is the perfect replacement for Tony. She's also a country girl at heart. But, golly, how can one person be in charge of a convent, an infirmary, a vineyard, a restaurant, a B&B, and a gift shop?"

"Yeah, but don't you teach at a grade school?"

"I've taught first grade for 15 years. I loved the kids and got a lot of satisfaction from watching how quickly they learn. But it's not hard to find someone to take my place. On the other hand, there aren't that many available Sisters to come here."

Cheryl added that the community and her family were very supportive of her decision to request an assignment on the east coast. Her parents knew that she could be sent wherever she was needed. "Quite honestly, mom and dad are used to us kids moving around. I think they enjoy visiting us, so they have an opportunity to tour the country."

"How about you, Cathy? What made you decide to ask to come here?" I asked.

"Cheryl talked me into it."

"I did not!"

"In a way, you did. You were so excited about our trip, then you wanted to stay and help Marian."

"You wanted to help her, too."

"That's true. We've all been friends since the novitiate. That's where you learn how to be a nun. My dad called it 'boot camp,' like from his Army days. I told him it wasn't the same, but he didn't care. Anyway, Marian's good at getting people to work together, but she doesn't have an accounting education like I do. I figured I could help her with the finances."

"Was it difficult to get a replacement for your classes at the college?"

"I kind of feel bad about that. They'll probably have to hire part time instructors. It's too late in the year to conduct a search for a full-time professor. Luckily, there are lots of CPA's who like to supplement their income with teaching."

Cathy explained that she'll oversee all financial aspects of the monastery. Cheryl will be in charge of the restaurant and B&B operations. Amanda will report to her. Marian will do the strategic planning for the whole institution and will focus on the infirmary.

Mention of the infirmary caught my attention, especially since Amanda told me that three of the older Sisters had died since she'd been working at the monastery.

Sister Cathy explained that there are now only six elderly Sisters receiving care. Four of them are in their eighties, and two are in their nineties. They all seemed to be doing well.

"Do you help Marian care for them?"

"Marian doesn't actually do any caregiving. She's more of an administrator, though she visits with each of the Sisters every day. Sister Elaine has a nursing degree, and she's assigned as nurse supervisor."

"I think I met her last Thanksgiving," I said. "But I don't believe I've ever had a lengthy conversation with her. How old is she?"

"Guess she's in her mid-fifties. She's been here forever. She kind of stays to herself when she's off-duty, which isn't very often. An aide comes in at night, so she can get some sleep."

I asked if more of the older Sisters in their community will be assigned to the infirmary. Cheryl told us that the merger with the mid-west branch had brought about some changes. The administrative team decided that any Sister needing long-term care in the future will go to the infirmary in St. Louis. Those who are here will stay until their passing.

"That seems wise," I said. "But what will you do with all that space? The mansion is so big for so few Sisters."

"Uh oh. Here she goes again," Betty said, rolling her eyes.

"I'm actually serious."

"That's Marian's job," Cheryl said. "She'll do the planning with input from our administration. You have to realize that the mansion wasn't built as a monastery. It was once the home of a wealthy couple who had no children."

"Get out of here. Really?"

"Sister Tony told us the history of the place before she left. Jonas Willard Smithfield and his wife, Hildegarde, bought the land and built the mansion in the 1920's, just before the stock market crash."

"Did they lose the estate in the Great Depression?"

"Not at all. JW was quite prosperous, despite the poor economic status of most Americans at that time. They hosted many notable dignitaries at their numerous parties and social events. We're not sure why, but they bequeathed the property to the Sisters, who took ownership in 1956."

"I wonder how he made his money," I said.

"Tony said he was an investor, and was immersed in a lot of market speculation," Cathy said. "He must have gotten out at the right time. I'd sure like to do some research on him."

"That'd be really interesting. I wonder if the couple left any documents or papers."

"I hope to explore. Anyone want to do some investigative work with me?"

"Not me," Betty and Cheryl said, almost at the same time.

"I'm game," I replied enthusiastically. "Sounds like fun."

"You want to spend these beautiful days in a dusty attic or basement?" Betty asked.

"You might have noticed that I'm prone to sunburn," I said. "In fact, I've about had enough for today. But I have plenty of time on my hands this week. Let me know when I can join you, Cathy."

"How about tomorrow morning after Mass? We could spend an hour or so in the basement, then get some lunch and still have lake time."

"Sure," I said as I began shaking my towel of sand. "I'll meet you at the gift shop. Now I'm going to sit in my porch rocking chair and read my book."

"You going to the restaurant for dinner tonight?" Betty asked.

"I don't think so. I brought a few microwavable meals. You going?"

"No, I'm going to call it an early night. I'll meet up with you at lunch tomorrow."

"Sounds like a plan."

Chapter 17

I had no idea what possessed me, but I decided to join the nuns for church services on Sunday morning. I guess I was hoping that Father Jim would be the minister. I liked hearing him preach.

I slid into the pew with Kate and Joe at the last part of the entrance hymn. Sister Cheryl was the first reader, sitting by the podium, and she winked when she saw me come in late. I leaned over to ask Joe where Amanda was. He whispered back that she had kitchen duty.

I was happy to see that Father Jim was saying the Mass. He's a tall man, clean-shaven, with graying hair and deep smile lines near his expressive eyes. He has a manner about him that draws young and old alike. When he delivered the homily, he spoke about the Prodigal Son in a way I'd never considered.

Father Jim told us about a homeless man named Leon who sometimes came by the soup kitchen for a meal. Leon was a veteran of the U.S. Army who fought in the Persian Gulf War back in the early 1990's. He was the oldest boy of a hardworking family, and his dad owned a small auto repair shop. As a teen, Leon learned his dad's trade, and the plan was that one day he'd join him in the business.

Leon was a changed man when he returned home from the war. He was forgetful, had terrible fatigue, strange rashes, joint pain, and shortness of breath. He also suffered from post-traumatic stress disorder, with terrifying flashbacks of seeing his buddies killed in a tank explosion. At the time, doctors could find no known diagnosis for his various symptoms. They're now lumped into the category of Gulf War Syndrome.

Leon's family tried to be supportive, but soon grew tired of his constant complaints of an illness that even the Pentagon didn't recognize. His brother called him crazy, arguing with him constantly. His father was frustrated when Leon didn't show up for work.

Leon eventually decided that his family would be better off if he weren't there. He moved to the city but couldn't hold a job long enough to provide the money to pay for an apartment. He lived out of his car for a while but ended up selling it because he couldn't afford the upkeep and insurance.

There was no specific treatment for Gulf War Syndrome. Leon self-medicated with alcohol, trying to keep his flashbacks at bay. Whiskey became his friend, more important to him than letting people into his life.

"When he was really hungry, or the cold winter weather got to him," Father Jim said, "Leon would arrive at the shelter. That's when I first met him, more than 10 years ago."

Father Jim told us that he started to look for Leon on the streets. When he'd find him, he'd encourage him to come in and get a hot meal and a shower. He gave Leon some small jobs and paid him for his work. Eventually, Leon began to trust Father Jim, and confided that he yearned to see his family. Father Jim helped him find a way to return home.

"I'd like to say that the homecoming was a happy one," Father Jim said. "His father greeted him warmly, telling him how much he was missed. His brother, on the other hand, was jealous of Leon's preferential treatment. He was cruel in his comments, and they often fought, even physically at times. Leon couldn't take it, and he returned to the streets."

I glanced around the chapel and saw that everyone was as mesmerized as I. Father Jim concluded his homily by saying, "The Prodigal Son is not just a story about the love of a father for his son. Its message is that we're loved fully and irrevocably, regardless of the foibles or mistakes we make in life; regardless of how we handle life's challenges. May we all find peace in the comfort of the Father's embrace."

I was deeply touched by the story about Leon, and my thoughts kept reverting to him throughout the remainder of the service. I wondered where he was now, and if there were new medications available to treat Gulf War Syndrome. I pondered how many other veterans might have similar stories, returning from combat as broken and forgotten. Before I knew it, we were singing the final hymn and Father Jim left the altar.

I walked with Kate and Joe back to the B&B and asked them about Leon. Joe mentioned that he'd met Leon a few times. Every so often, he came to see Father Jim. Apparently, he's still homeless. We all agreed that we'd think about Leon whenever we heard the story of the Prodigal Son.

When we got to the monastery entrance, Joe asked if I was coming to breakfast. Kate excused herself, saying that she'd run ahead to lend Amanda a hand.

"No, I'm meeting up with Sister Cathy at the gift shop. We plan to explore the basement. See if we might find information about the guy who built the mansion."

"Cool. You think I can tag along?"

"I don't see why not. Let's check it out."

Chapter 18

Sister Cathy was already at the gift shop, helping Dolores open up for business. When Joe asked to join us to explore the basement, Dolores was particularly encouraging. She wanted him to bring up another carton of wine. It had been a big seller through the weekend.

Inside the elevator, Cathy pressed the 4-digit code for the basement, explaining that Tony had wanted the lower level off-limits to any visitors. When the new elevator was installed, she requested the code panel next to the button to the basement.

"Guests of the B&B can use the elevator to get to their rooms upstairs, but can't explore the basement," Cathy added.

"Makes sense," I said, nodding my agreement. "After all, it's where Dolores stores all of the items she's purchased for the gift shop."

"Also where the Sisters keep their personal belongings. We have a stairway to the basement on the convent side of the mansion, near the chapel. Of course, that's private."

"Was there always an elevator on this side?" Joe asked.

"I'm not sure. The Smithfield's were probably wealthy enough to have had one back in the 1920's, but most likely it had been updated at some point after the Sisters took ownership."

"Maybe we'll find blueprints or something," Joe noted as the elevator door opened. "But I want to see the bowling alley."

The basement is the full footprint of the mansion, making it an enormous expanse. Sister Tony had told us that there was a bowling alley, and sure enough, one long lane and a gutter took up much of the length of the main wing. It had a wood finish, with ten pins neatly arranged on their designated positions.

I remembered reading somewhere that it wasn't unusual to find bowling alleys in homes of the wealthy. Of course, those vintage alleys didn't have mechanisms to automatically reset the pins. Players had to do that themselves.

"Wow! This is cool," Joe said, checking it out. "Wonder where the bowling balls are kept."

"I don't know," Cathy replied. "Maybe in those cabinets along the wall? Actually, that might be a good place to look for any old papers, too."

"Don't you think the early nuns might have cleaned out the basement long ago?"

"Maybe, but we don't come down here too often unless we want to store things. It's pretty dusty, and there are lots of spiders."

We walked around to get the lay of the land. Cartons of wine, items for the gift shop, and Charlie's belongings were piled neatly in the section under the B&B. At the other end of the basement, a number of steamer trunks were lined up on pallets in the area under the chapel. Cathy explained that they belonged to the older Sisters.

"Back in the day, the Sisters were permitted to keep only the things that fit in their trunks. When they were transferred, their trunks went with them."

"You've got to be kidding," Joe said.

"We take a vow of poverty," Cathy said. "It's a little more loosely interpreted now, but we still aim to be detached from worldly goods. Just use what we need to sustain our ministry."

"That's got to be tough," Joe said. "I can't imagine trying to fit all my stuff into one little trunk."

Sister Cathy suggested that we focus on the main section of the basement under the convent. The trunk room would have nothing from the original owners. She wanted to check out the cabinets that lined the entire front wall of the mansion. She assumed they were probably part of the original construction.

It was obvious that the Smithfield's spared no expense. Made of cedar wood, they were built from floor to ceiling. As we opened each of them, we noticed that some of the cabinets had shelving. Others were wardrobes with poles across the top that could be used for hanging clothes.

Joe was ecstatic when he found two bowling balls and an extra pin. "Look at these balls. They're different sizes, but they only have two finger holes."

"Maybe the large one was for JW and the smaller one for his wife," Cathy said as she rummaged through another cabinet.

"Man, they're heavy," Joe said. "I don't know what they're made of, but I don't think I'd be able to play many frames with these. You mind if I try one out?"

"Go ahead," Cathy said. "See if you can get a strike."

Joe chose the smaller of the two balls and positioned himself at the end of the lane. We watched as he swung the ball and let it go. Four pins went down. He went to the back end to retrieve the ball and began again. Three more pins went down.

Joe suggested that I give it a try. He reset the pins and returned the ball to me. My first attempt was a gutter ball, but I got two pins on my next throw.

Cathy took a turn but didn't do much better. She and I went back to exploring the cabinets while Joe attempted to improve his score.

"We need a ladder," Cathy said, gazing around the room. "I can't see if there's anything on the high shelves."

Joe offered to check the storage area under the B&B. As he stood from resetting pins, he ended up flat on the floor.

"Are you OK?" I asked. "What happened?"

"I don't know. I tripped over something. I guess I can be a little clumsy."

"Do that again," Cathy said.

We looked at her like she was nuts. "You want him to fall again?" I asked.

"Of course not. See if you can find what made you trip, Joe. I heard a noise in one of the cabinets."

"What kind of noise?"

"I'm not sure. It was some kind of click, like a mechanism of some sort."

^^^

Joe and I both checked the area around the bowling alley. There wasn't anything that could have caused Joe to trip. He got down on all fours, sweeping the floor with his hands. Finally, Joe felt a small raised nodule, almost imperceptible to the eye.

"How about this?" he asked as he pushed it. Sure enough, we all heard a muffled click.

"Do it again," Cathy said, opening more cabinet doors.

Joe repeatedly pressed the bump until Cathy found the cabinet with the most pronounced sound. It came from one of the tall wardrobe closets, but it was empty.

"There's nothing here," she said in dismay.

Cathy felt along all of the seams of the closet, searching for some type of hinge or mechanism. We took turns doing the same, but the wardrobe was intact.

"This is going to drive me crazy," Cathy said. "Show me what you tripped on, Joe, so I can show Marian and Cheryl. We'll have to come down here later, because I promised to meet them for lunch."

"Yeah, I've got to relieve Amanda," Joe said. "If you want, I can help after my shift."

Joe showed Cathy the slight protrusion in the floor, then pushed a carton of wine to the elevator. We headed to the dining room, still stymied with our find.

"Any ghosts down there?" Betty teased when I arrived at her table.

"Possibly," I laughed. "You been waiting long?"

"Only a few minutes. I told Kate I'd wait 'til you got here before ordering."

"I'm going to go wash up. It's mighty dusty down there. Get me a hamburger and Coke if Kate comes by while I'm gone."

When I returned, Amanda was sitting with Betty. Joe had relieved Amanda in the kitchen, then after a brief respite, she'd give Kate a break.

Amanda and Betty were both curious about our findings in the basement. I told them about the old bowling balls, and the bump in the floor that Joe had tripped on.

"Joe mentioned that it made some kind of noise in the cabinet," Amanda said.

"It's really strange," I said. "Except for the pole to hang clothes, there's nothing there."

"So, is the bowling alley cool?"

"It is. In fact, we each tried to bowl but it wasn't easy. The balls are really heavy. I wish I'd brought my laptop this week, so I could research vintage bowling alleys in mansions. I'd like to know what those balls are made of."

"You could check it out with the computer in the parlor," Amanda said. "The nuns put one there last week for the guests to use."

"That's a fabulous addition," I said as Kate arrived with our food. I was already planning my time. Betty just rolled her eyes.

"Aren't we going to the lake after lunch?" she asked while reaching for the ketchup.

"Of course. It's a gorgeous day, perfect for lounging."

"I wouldn't mind a canoe ride. You up for it?"

"Definitely."

Betty and Amanda laughed, knowing that my reply was more sardonic than sincere. It's not that I didn't enjoy a peaceful glide across the water, but paddling was a whole different story. It's pretty demanding exercise. Come to think of it, I wasn't great with the balancing part either.

"The canoe's going to be in great demand this afternoon," Amanda said, her brown eyes teasing.

"Why's that?"

"Father Jim told me that he was planning to use the canoe this afternoon. He's staying at the B&B until tomorrow night."

"No problem," Betty said. "We can share."

"Joe, Kate, and I have some free time between lunch and dinner service. We're going to the lake, too."

"The more, the merrier," I said. "Don't forget to pick up a visor at the gift shop."

"Very funny! I'll catch you later. Time for me to relieve Kate."

Chapter 19

Betty and I spread our towels on the beach, then lathered on the suntan lotion. Amanda had been right about the canoe. Father Jim beat us to it. We sat watching his easy strokes, leaving smooth ripples created each time his paddles propelled him through the water.

"Hope you're not too disappointed," I remarked, donning my hat and sunglasses.

"We'll have plenty of time this week for a canoe ride."

I nodded my agreement, recognizing that the downside of more guests at the monastery meant sharing the amenities. It wasn't a bad thing, just different.

"So, other than the three of you playing around with the bowling balls in the basement, you didn't find anything of worth down there?" Betty asked, interrupting my train of thought.

I told Betty about the whole wall of built-in cedar wood cabinets. "They go from floor to ceiling. We were going to get a ladder to try to see if anything's in any of the high cabinets, but that's when Joe tripped. The lower cabinets had all been cleaned out at some point in time."

"Sounds like a wild goose chase to me. You might be able to find information at the county library or historical society."

"Probably, but now we have to figure out why something in the floor make a clicking noise in an empty closet."

Betty just shook her head, gazing across the lake. I knew she was thinking that I get too involved in this place, but I enjoy a good mystery. It might be fun to discover the hidden secrets of the couple who bequeathed their estate to the nuns.

Of course, there probably wasn't anything covert about the original owners of the mansion. Quite simply, the button on the floor was close to the bowling alley and may have triggered some type of mechanism to retrieve balls or reset the pins. My curiosity was merely clashing with my better sense to mind my own business.

"Did you sleep in today?" Betty asked, changing the topic.

"No, I went to church services."

"What's with all this religious stuff? You going to be a nun?"

"Very funny. I just like to hear Father Jim preach. He says stuff that makes me think. And it makes me feel good."

I told her about the homily of the prodigal son and Leon, the homeless man. Though I knew that he still felt the ravages of Gulf War Syndrome, I wondered if there might be a newer medication that could help Leon live a normal life.

"He might think that his life is just perfect the way it is," Betty said. "Don't get me wrong. I advocate for people down on their luck. It's just that I've learned that some folks don't want interference from a do-gooder."

Betty and I heard the sound of the canoe being beached at the same time. Father Jim dragged it out of the water, and we waved for him to join us.

"That was a great workout," he said as he put his towel next to mine. "You ladies going to take a ride around the lake?"

"We were thinking about it," I said. "I was just telling Betty about Leon."

"Sad story," Father Jim said. "Wish I could figure out a way to help him. He's a really good guy."

"Betty thinks he might like being homeless."

"I'm not sure that he does. But he doesn't want to be tied down with a lot of personal belongings. Quite honestly, there aren't a lot of opportunities for an African American veteran with PTSD and Gulf War Syndrome. Leon doesn't want to be beholding to anyone. You need money to own property, and you have to work to earn money."

"You know, Charlie was once homeless," I said. "He found peace and contentment here, living in a poustinia and taking responsibility for the grounds. He was a big help to the Sisters. I wonder if it would be an option for Leon as well."

"You have such an imagination!" Betty said.

"I don't know why, but the idea just popped into my head. Just think about it. The nuns are going to need assistance now that Charlie went to St. Louis."

"That's not a bad idea," Father Jim said. "I think a cabin in the woods would be an ideal place for Leon. I know he's a hard worker when he can work. He'd have the flexibility to design his own schedule as groundskeeper."

"Yeah, but the Sisters don't have the money to hire someone," Betty said.

"Maybe they could set up the same type of arrangement they had with Charlie," I said. "You know, like room and board for his work, and perhaps a little stipend."

"My foundation might be able to assist with the stipend," Father Jim said, nodding as he gave some thought to the idea. "After all, it's our mission to help people get back on their feet. I'll ask Sister Marian if there might be an opportunity for Leon here at the monastery."

"Definitely do that," I said. "I don't know the guy, but I think it would be a perfect arrangement. He could even cut the grass, so they don't need to get goats."

"Or he could take care of the goats, so Amanda doesn't have to do it," Betty said. We all laughed.

"I have a feeling that Marian's going to get a few goats regardless of what we suggest," Father Jim said. "Now you girls better get in that canoe before Amanda, Joe, and Kate get here. If not, you'll miss your chance."

Chapter 20

After our jaunt around the lake, Betty and I decided we'd had enough sun for the day. We grabbed our stuff, telling Father Jim to enjoy the rest of the afternoon. He said he planned to do a little reading, then take a snooze depending on when the young crowd arrived.

Betty and I parted ways on the path to the cabins but not before arranging to meet at the restaurant for supper. That fit into my schedule quite nicely. I wanted to take a quick shower and change into a nice pair of capris and matching blouse, then do a little research on the monastery computer.

A few guests were in the gift shop, others were checking out after their weekend at the B&B. Dolores and Julie were both busy, so I just waved as I passed by. The lounge was empty. I booted up the computer and googled Jonas Willard Smithfield.

There were a number of references about Mr. Smithfield and his wife, Hildegarde. I clicked on the various links and found that JW was born of ordinary means in 1878. As a young man in the post-civil war northeast, he worked jobs in iron mills, then moved to the steel industry.

Jonas was greatly influenced by Carnegie's writings, and he modeled his business acumen on Carnegie's principles of innovation and fiscal management. He eventually became CEO of a large steel mill. According to what I read, JW made millions when the railroads converted iron rails to steel rails.

JW married Hildegarde in 1913, a young woman he met and fell in love with while travelling through Germany prior to WWI. Her parents were wealthy landowners whose vineyards were acclaimed throughout the wine-making region. Although they initially settled in the city, JW promised to build a country estate where Hildegarde could start her own vineyard.

By the early 1920's, JW had increased his wealth by speculation in the stock market. A smart investor, he managed to move out of the market and into real estate before the great crash. Apparently, that was the time frame that the Smithfield's completed construction on their mansion and permanently moved to the rural countryside.

Hildegarde planted prized grape vines that had been sent to her from her parents' vineyard, one historical website noted. She became known by the farming locals to make delicious jams and jellies as the grapes matured.

There was some suggestion in one article I read that JW might have been involved in bootlegging during the prohibition. Despite an investigation into the matter, no evidence had been discovered.

Instead, the couple became known for their generosity to many charities and were considered part of the higher echelon of society. Distinguished guests often visited, including Grace Coolidge, First Lady, and numerous members of Congress.

I was totally engrossed in my research until Betty's voice startled me. Looking up, I saw her standing in the doorway of the parlor with a teasing expression.

"What are you doing?"

"Look what I've discovered about the Smithfield's," I said, showing her my notes.

"You're like a dog with a bone."

"I think it's interesting. Picture it. Dignitaries arriving for grand soirees, the ladies in designer gowns on the arms of their wealthy husbands. They may have even stayed in the rooms that are now the B&B."

"Maybe. Could be why the Smithfield's had such a grand staircase near the foyer. I wonder if they had any servants."

"I haven't found any information about that, but I'm sure they would have. It's kind of strange to me that there's mention of Hildegarde making jams and jellies. You'd think that'd be the job of the hired help."

"Knowing you, you'll keep at it until you have all of the pieces fitting together. Come on. Let's eat before they close up shop for the evening."

^^^

Reluctantly, I shut down the computer and put my notes into my pocket. When we arrived at the restaurant, there were only a few guests and a couple of Sisters scattered among the tables. A sign at the entrance noted that we should seat ourselves. Betty suggested that we join Cathy and Cheryl as it looked that they, too, had recently arrived.

Cheryl offered to take our order to the kitchen since Kate typically left early on Sunday evenings. While we waited for our meals, I asked Cathy if she and the Sisters had a chance to do any further exploration in the basement.

"We were tied up in a meeting with Father Jim."

"Was it about Leon?"

"Actually, it was," Cathy replied. "Father Jim mentioned your conversation at the lake. Seems like you guys concocted a scheme."

"Vicki's always got something up her sleeve," Betty said.

"What did you decide?" I asked.

Sister Cathy told us that Father Jim's going to try to locate Leon and see if he'd be interested in being the groundskeeper. If he is, the nuns will interview him to determine if they think he could do the job.

I suggested that Leon could live in Charlie's cabin. It's the farthest one into the woods, and I thought he'd like it there.

"Do you know this guy?" Cheryl asked.

"No. I just have a good feeling about him. And I trust Father Jim's judgment of character."

"Time will tell," Cathy said as Cheryl and Amanda arrived with our meals.

"Looks like you forgot to wear a hat at the lake today," I said to Amanda as she put my plate in front of me. "Got a little sunburn, eh?"

"Yeah, but we had a great time. Joe said we need another canoe, or maybe a kayak. Then we could have races on the lake. That'd be cool."

"Save your shekels so you can donate one."

"Very funny," Amanda retorted. "What shekels?"

Though we all laughed at Amanda's expression, I agreed that we needed another canoe. In fact, I offered to provide the funding if the Sisters were interested.

Without hesitation, Sister Cathy took me up on my offer. Since I had no idea what features were important when buying a canoe, nor where a sporting goods store might be located, I suggested that Amanda and Joe do the leg work.

"Awesome!" Amanda said with a broad smile. "Wait 'til I tell Joe. He's going to be mighty happy."

"The two of you can finish early this evening," Cheryl said to Amanda. "We have no other reservations for dinner, and everyone else has eaten."

"Sounds good to me. We'll start to clean up now. You guys want any dessert?"

Sister Cheryl suggested that Amanda bring out anything that she wanted to finish up. I was hoping there'd be a piece of coconut cream pie in the mix. When she was out of earshot, Cheryl told us what a godsend Amanda has been.

"She hasn't had any meltdowns?" I asked.

"Well, maybe just a few," Cathy said with a chuckle. "But Joe keeps her on an even keel, and Kate's a great support on the weekends. Cheryl also tries to give Amanda some breaks, so she doesn't get burned out. It seems to be working."

While we were eating, I recounted what I'd learned about JW and his wife. Even though I had only scratched the surface, I discovered that the Smithfield's were generous philanthropists who were well-liked in the higher social circles.

"I guess that's kind of amazing given the time-frame that they lived here," Cathy said. "The Roaring 20's was a unique period in U.S. History. The wealthy seemed to be corrupt in many ways, and many of them got richer preying on those who had lost everything when the stock market crashed in '29."

"Wasn't that also around the time of prohibition?" Betty asked.

"Yeah," Cheryl replied. "Gangsters like Al Capone made millions bootlegging. Speakeasies were set up so that people could buy illegal alcohol. Even home-made moonshine was rampant."

"Maybe that's why a few historical websites mentioned Hildegarde's passion for making jellies and jams. Surely a vineyard would raise red flags," I said.

"From what you've told us," Cathy said, "the Smithfield's held a fine reputation and were charitable benefactors. Doesn't sound like they were involved in any corruption."

"I've only begun my research, but I didn't come across anything that would indicate that JW's wealth was achieved through schemes or illegal activities. One article noted that he was investigated at least once, maybe because of the vineyards but, overall, the articles were very positive."

Sister Cathy suggested that we continue our exploration of the basement in the morning. She wanted to investigate the top shelves of the cabinets. Betty said she wasn't interested, and Cheryl's afraid of spiders. I agreed to meet Cathy at 10:30 by the elevator.

"What's at 10:30?" Amanda asked as she brought in the desserts.

"We're going to explore the basement some more," I said.

"Can I come, too?"

"Of course," Cathy said.

"Awesome! Joe's going to be bummed out that he has to work at the diner, but I haven't seen the bowling alley yet."

Amanda went to the kitchen to help Joe with clean-up. When she returned to the dining room, she checked out the last few customers. As we finished our desserts, Betty and I gave her our credit cards so that she could close out the register.

Joe greeted us as he began to bus the tables. I told him how much I enjoyed my meal.

"I heard that Amanda's going to help you in the basement tomorrow," he said.

"She said you have to work at the diner."

"Yeah. But it's OK. She's going to try to knock down more pins than I did. Don't let her cheat. And, by the way, Vicki, it's awesome that you're going to buy us another canoe."

Chapter 21

Amanda and Sister Cathy were waiting by the elevator when I arrived the next morning. I greeted Sister Marian as she was leaving the gift shop, and told her of our plans to explore the basement again. She said she wanted to join us so she could see for herself the curious contraption we had found. Marian made some ghostly noises for good measure.

Cathy showed Marian the button in the basement floor, while I got Amanda to help me find the ladder in the storage area. "I can't imagine how Joe managed to trip on that thing," Marian said. "It barely protrudes from the floor."

"He's kind of clumsy sometimes," Amanda said. "Let me see it."

Amanda pushed on the nodule and we all heard the click. Cathy showed Marian the wardrobe with the most pronounced sound. Marian ran her fingers around all of the closet seams. She agreed that nothing seemed movable. In fact, she noted, the click would be barely noticeable if the closet had been filled with clothes.

I set up the ladder, and Cathy began exploring the top cabinet shelves. Amanda challenged Marian to see who could knock down the most pins. I showed them where the bowling balls were located, and Amanda retrieved the smaller of the two.

"Joe's right," Amanda said, examining the vintage relic. "These bowling balls are really heavy. And they only have two finger holes. Weird."

"I meant to research what the balls are made of," I said. "I know that JW worked in the iron and steel industries. Maybe he used leftover iron to make the balls."

"I don't think so," Marian said. "They'd be rusty by now."

Amanda positioned herself and threw the ball down the alley. She got five pins down, and went to retrieve the ball. She took her aim again, and knocked down two more pins.

"This is ridiculous," Amanda remarked as she trudged the length of the alley to re-set the pins and get the ball. "Who'd ever want to bowl if they had to do so much work in order to play?"

"They probably had servants stationed at the pin deck to put the pins in place and return the ball," I said.

Sister Marian took her turn, but didn't do any better than Amanda. She retrieved the ball, and repositioned the pins. In the meantime, Cathy stretched as high as she could maneuver on the ladder and reached far back in a top cabinet. Suddenly, she called out, "I found something!"

"What is it?" we all echoed excitedly.

"Seems like some kind of notebook. I have to be careful. It's falling apart."

Cathy handed me the fragile document while she climbed down the ladder. When I returned it to her, she gently opened the cover. The others huddled around us.

"It looks like a ledger," Cathy said. "I think we'd better take it upstairs so we can put it on a table. We shouldn't handle it too much."

^^^

Leaving the ladder in place, the four of us returned to the main floor. Marian, Cathy, and I took the ledger to the parlor. Amanda reluctantly headed to the kitchen to get ready for lunch service.

Sister Cathy gingerly placed the notebook on the game table. It looked like an old-fashioned composition booklet that could have been used in a vintage classroom. The cover used a type of heavy stock paper, not cardboard, while the sewn pages seemed to be made of newsprint. All of it was yellowed with age, the inside pages crumbling with the slightest touch.

We all gazed over her shoulder at the first inside page as Cathy gently opened the cover. Ornate cursive writing had been penned in ink, and five columns had been drawn with a ruler.

The first column looked to be first and last name initials. The second column was dated. The third column contained a numeral, and the fourth seemed to note a monetary value. The fifth column was some type of tally.

"This is definitely a ledger," Cathy observed.

"Maybe it's a record from constructing the mansion," I said. "The initials could be the names of contractors, and the other columns might indicate what was paid."

"I don't think so," Cathy said. "Why use initials? If it was about construction, you'd have the type of service indicated in a column, like plumbing, stone masonry, electricity."

"How about a record of Hildegarde's jams and jellies?" Marian asked.

"Could be," Cathy said. "The third column could indicate the number of jars sold, and the fourth column could be the price per jar. The last column definitely looks like accounts receivable."

"Yeah, but look at the prices in column four," I argued. "They range from $3.00 to $8.00. I can't imagine that a jar of jelly was that expensive."

"The ledger's definitely cryptic," Cathy said. "I'd say that JW was buying bootleg spirits, or he was selling them. That's my guess. Either way, he wouldn't want to get caught or implicate anyone else. That's probably why he used only initials."

"Wow!" I exclaimed. "Has there ever been any mention of the first nuns here finding a still?"

"I haven't heard anything like that," Marian replied. "I could ask the Sisters in the infirmary."

I suggested that the county historical society might also be able to shed some light on our find. If anything, perhaps they had records of local residents fined for illegal bootlegging in the 1920's.

Sister Cathy and I decided that the following afternoon would be a good opportunity for us to pay a visit to the historical society, especially since the weather forecast predicted rain. I offered to drive, figuring my GPS could guide us.

"Have at it, girls," Marian said with a chuckle. She offered to take the notebook to the convent, while the rest of us went to the dining room. I had a feeling that Betty was probably waiting for me there.

Chapter 22

Betty was having lunch with Dolores and Julie when I arrived. Sister Cheryl and Amanda were also eating, but it looked like they were engrossed in menu planning for the week. Betty waved me over to join her table. She told me to grab a plate and make a sandwich from the fixings on the side table.

I made a ham and cheese on rye and got myself a bottle of cold water before I sat down. "Sorry I'm late."

"No problem. We were just chatting about the gift shop," Betty said. "Sister Julie's planning to make a couple of batches of strawberry jam this afternoon. Her jellies have been flying off the shelves."

"We had to order several cases of jelly jars," Dolores said. "But it was worth it. Even with the cost of the strawberries and jars, we're making a good profit from the sales."

I told the Sisters that I learned Hildegarde Smithfield also was known for her jellies and jams. I suggested they might want to highlight some of the historical aspects of the early days of the mansion in their gift shop display.

"That's not a bad idea," Julie said. "I found the recipe I use for the grape jelly among some boxes in the basement. It was yellowed with age and written in script, but I made a copy of it years ago."

My ears picked up. "Where are these boxes you found?"

"I put them in one of the old steamer trunks," Julie said. "I remember that the trunk belonged to Sister Casimir, who died when I was a novice. She was such a sweetheart. You remember her, Dolores?"

"Sure, but where's your brain? Haven't you heard Cathy talking about looking for old stuff in the basement?"

"I actually forgot about the cartons until Vicki mentioned Hildegarde's jelly. What's the big deal?"

"The big deal is that you can immerse yourself in your own little world," Dolores said. "What's in the cartons?"

"Just a bunch of old papers and notebooks. Guess I put them aside when we were cleaning the basement because there seemed to be some recipes that I might be able to use. I totally forgot about them."

"Well, you'd better find the boxes and bring them to the community room. We can go through them after supper and see what's there."

"I have a feeling you just made Vicki a very happy lady," Betty said. "She'll probably want to join you this evening."

I agreed that I was curious, but said I wouldn't want to intrude on the Sisters' private time. Surely Sister Cathy would share anything of interest.

Dolores wondered why we were so intrigued about the history of the monastery. I told her about the conversation that Betty and I had with Cheryl and Cathy at the lake.

"The other day we were chatting about how few Sisters are here, and that the infirmary will be relocated in the future. I remember asking what you'd do with all the extra space. Cheryl said that Sister Tony told her what she knew about the original owners who were childless, so Cathy and I thought it'd be fun to find out more about the Smithfield's."

"They had servants," Dolores said, raising an eyebrow. "They weren't rambling around this place all alone."

"Probably," I agreed. "But I haven't found any mention of them in my research. I wonder where they were housed."

"Third floor of the main wing," Dolores replied without hesitation. "There used to be a back staircase to the kitchen. We converted the upper level to a dormitory when there were a lot of novices and postulants. Now it's back to individual rooms. And the elevator's where the stairs had been located."

"We lost a lot of space up there when the ductwork was installed for central air conditioning," Julie said. "I can only imagine how hot it must have been on the third floor."

"You can only imagine?" Dolores retorted. "We slept up there, for heaven's sake. I remember that it was stifling in the summer."

"Yeah, that's true," Julie chuckled. "Those were the good old days!"

I was enjoying the banter between the two Sisters when Amanda arrived at our table. She looked like the proverbial Cheshire cat as she inquired about my plans for the afternoon.

"Betty and I intend to go to the lake. Why?"

"Cheryl just gave me the night off. How'd you like to go canoe shopping? There are no guests other than the two of you, and the nuns can have leftovers for supper."

"I thought Joe wanted to pick out the canoe."

"I just texted him. He'll be here by 4:00, and the four of us could go to a sporting goods store, and maybe out to dinner."

I looked at Betty and she began to laugh. "I think it's a great plan," she said. "Besides, you're the one with shekels."

"You've got shekels, too."

"Not as many as you. I'm a poor public defender."

"Yeah, right," I said, rolling my eyes.

Julie and Dolores sided with Betty. They, too, thought it was a great idea. I took some time before responding, just to drive Amanda crazy. Finally, I agreed.

"Awesome!" Amanda said. "Joe's going to drive because he can tie the canoe to the roof of his car. We'll meet you in the parking lot at 4:00 p.m."

I glanced over at Cheryl. She was laughing, but gave me the thumbs up sign. I think she instigated this plot, and everyone else was in cahoots.

Chapter 23

Joe and Amanda were waiting by his car when Betty and I got
to the parking lot. We had found a sporting goods store at the
outlet mall, and I purchased the canoe that Joe picked out. It
was a two-seater that looked rather sturdy, with a striking red
shell. The best part for me was that it was on sale.

Betty treated us all to dinner at the food court, which was
more convenient than pulling into a restaurant parking lot with
a canoe on the roof of the car. Amanda and Joe finished eating
first, then took the car around to the store's loading dock to
begin tying the canoe. Betty and I took a leisurely walk through
the mall to meet them there.

"Have you talked to Charlie lately?" Betty asked when we
paused to glance at the display window for the Talbots outlet.

"Actually, I did. I called him last night to see if he knew
anything about the nodule in the mansion's basement floor."

"How'd that go?"

"The conversation or the answer to my question?"

"Both."

"Pretty good. You know Charlie's not a big gabber unless
there's something specific to chat about. The basement was a
good starting point."

"Did he know anything about the mechanism?"

"No. He said he never saw it, but he'd never paid much attention to the bowling alley. Only time he went down there was to store his stuff or bring up cartons for the nuns."

"Did he have any idea what the clicking sound could be?"

"Not really. He said he'd ask Tony when he saw her."

"Does he see her often?"

"I don't think so. Reading between the lines, I thought he seemed frustrated that she was so busy with her new position. He didn't actually come out and say that, but he mentioned that she's always in meetings."

"Where's he living?"

"Some boarding house. I don't think he likes it. Said it's on a busy street, and the walls are paper thin."

"He has a job, doesn't he?"

"Yeah, he's working as a custodian at a grade school. He didn't talk about it, but I can't imagine that he'd want to clean classrooms and bathrooms. Of course, it's probably easier now because only summer classes are running, but it was his choice to go there."

Betty nodded her agreement as we continued our stroll. I smiled at a young couple pushing a baby carriage, noting their proud stance. They must have been new parents, out to show off their first child.

The outlet mall was like a maze, but we located the exit closest to the sporting goods store. It didn't take much longer to get to the loading dock.

"Did you tell Charlie about Leon?" Betty asked. "That you might have found his replacement as groundskeeper?"

"No. I didn't want to rub salt in his wounds. Besides, we don't really know if Leon will work out. I wouldn't want Charlie to think that he has no option to return to the monastery."

"You still have feelings for Charlie, don't you?"

"Yeah, I guess so. After I hung up last night I was thinking about how much fun it would be for the two of us to solve the mystery of the mansion."

"You could still work on it together from a distance."

"It's not the same. But, I must say, I enjoyed chatting with him about it."

"He's a good guy. I think he'll be back."

"We'll see. But don't say anything about my conversation with Charlie in front of Amanda. I don't want to open any can of worms."

We arrived at the loading dock just as Joe and Amanda finished tying the canoe to the roof of the car. Joe was checking all of the ropes to make sure the canoe was tightly fastened.

"Perfect timing," Amanda said. "Let's get going. Joe and I want to test it out on the lake before it gets dark."

Joe dropped Betty and me off near my cabin since it was closest to the road. We didn't dawdle because I knew Amanda and Joe had planned to paddle around the lake, and dusk was approaching.

I invited Betty for a cup of tea, but she said she was tired and wanted to hit the sack early. We decided to meet for lunch at the restaurant the next day. She planned to let me know if she'd join Sister Cathy and me at the county historical society.

"Remember, it's supposed to rain tomorrow," I said. "You don't want to be stuck in your cabin on a rainy day."

"I'm quite content to relax with my book."

"Well, think about it. I'd enjoy your company."

Chapter 24

I had second thoughts about walking over to the monastery for lunch the next day. It was pouring, and my umbrella was in the trunk of my car. Betty must have been thinking the same thing, because she called me on my cell phone to tell me that Sister Julie was going to pick us up in the golf cart.

"I heard your shopping trip last night was successful," Julie said as she rounded the bend to the monastery's *porte couchère*. "We really appreciate your donation of the new canoe for the lake."

"Glad I could help. It'll certainly get as much use as the one that Jeff donated last summer."

"Without a doubt. We've been getting a lot of guests. In fact, we're booked solid for the weekend."

"Do you want us to leave before Saturday?" Betty asked.

"Not at all," Julie said. "You paid for your week, fair and square. Upcoming reservations won't check in until after your departure. I'm saving Charlie's cabin in case the groundskeeper position works out."

"Did Father Jim find Leon?" I asked.

"He did. They're arriving today. We plan to interview the guy after lunch. Father Jim's homily about the prodigal son was very touching, so I'm looking forward to meeting Leon."

"It sounds like Cathy's going to be tied up this afternoon," I said, trying not to show my disappointment. "We were hoping to go to the historical society."

"I know. Unfortunately, we're going to need her here."

"Looks like you're going to have to come with me," I said to Betty as we walked into the mansion.

"Guess I do." She didn't look too happy about it.

Sandwich fixings were again set up at the sideboard in the dining room. It really was the most resourceful way of using Amanda's time during lunch service. And folks seemed to like it.

Betty and I each made a tuna salad wrap and grabbed a bag of chips. We sat with Sister Cheryl and Amanda. Father Jim and Leon were sitting with Marian and Cathy.

"How's the new canoe?" I asked Amanda.

"Awesome!"

"I'm glad to see you didn't drown in the dark last night."

"We didn't stay out late. We just tested it, then covered it with a tarp. Good thing we did. It's pouring out there today."

"Wouldn't want it to get wet," Betty said. We all laughed.

Amanda told us that she and Joe had made chocolate chip cookies when they got in last night, then watched a movie. It was some horror flick that Amanda didn't like. She said they almost had a big fight about it. I knew that Amanda doesn't like scary things, but she can usually hold her own in an argument.

I decided to change the subject. "Have you heard from your grandfather lately?"

"Yeah, I called him the other day. I don't think he's very happy."

"Why not?"

"I told him that the nuns are going to interview someone for his old job here."

"How'd he react?" I asked.

"He got quiet. Maybe I shouldn't have told him, but I thought it might make him want to come back before it's too late."

"He's always got a home here, Amanda," Cheryl said. "Even if we decide to hire Leon, there's still plenty of work for Charlie."

"Well, someone should tell him that."

"You can tell him the next time you talk to him."

"I will. Besides, you might not like Leon."

"We might not, but it doesn't matter," Cheryl said. "What do you think of him?"

"He's all right, I guess. I mean like I only talked to him for a minute, but I know he tends to disappear when things don't go his way. We don't need that around here."

"If the nuns decide to give him a chance," I said, "you might be able to help him."

"Like how?"

"You've worked at the shelter. You've seen the struggles that people face when they're homeless."

"Yeah, but I'm not a counselor. That's Father Jim's job."

"Seems to me you've dealt with a lot of stuff in your life," Betty countered. "Probably all Leon would need is to know that he's accepted, and he's got someone to show him the ropes."

Amanda was about to respond when Sister Marian and her guests made their way to our table. Marian introduced us to Leon, and we all extended our welcome.

Leon's a tall African American man with broad shoulders and thick muscles. I could see his military training in how he carried himself. He's clean-shaven, and his short hair is speckled with gray. He seemed a little uncomfortable about being in the spotlight, but he shook our hands warmly.

"Pleased to meet you all," he said.

"Likewise," I replied with a welcoming smile.

"We're going to interview Leon for the groundskeeper position today," Sister Cathy said. "Unfortunately I won't be able to honor our plans to go to the historical society."

"I understand. It's not a problem. Betty's going to come with me." Betty rolled her eyes.

"OK, she's not happy about it," I said, "but she knows how to humor me."

"We should make you our archivist," Cathy said. "Hope the historical society has information about JW and his wife. Find some interesting tidbits about our Smithfield benefactors."

"We'll do our best," I said. "And the best to you, too, Leon. Good luck with your interview."

Chapter 25

Sister Julie was kind enough to drive Betty and me to my car in the parking lot. Despite the rain, I was excited to get on the road. I put the location for the historical society into my GPS, and was busy listening to the drone of "Turn left in 100 yards."

"I wonder if Sister Cathy was serious about making you an archivist," Betty commented as soon as we got moving.

"She was just using a figure of speech."

"Maybe. Maybe not. It might be something you could do in retirement. Would you be interested?"

"I like researching, but I don't think I'd enjoy cataloguing. Besides, I wouldn't know what types of information should be archived. What I'd really like to do is what the Sisters are doing as we speak. Interviewing candidates for a position."

"That's your current job. Choose something different."

"Why?"

"Retirement should fun. Take advantage of a new stage of life that would allow you to do things you've never had time to do before."

"What, like take up painting or something?"

"Sure, if that would interest you."

"I wouldn't be any good at it."

"Who cares? You could express your inner feelings."

"My inner feelings are just fine where they are. Why are you picking on me?"

"I'm not picking on you. I just asked if you'd want to be an archivist for the nuns. That's all."

"Well, I don't."

"That's OK," Betty said. "How about running the B&B?

"What's this sudden attention to my retirement?"

"I'm just throwing out ideas you might not have thought about."

"I'm certainly not interested in living my final years at a monastery."

"I thought you liked the place. I mean, after all, you get really into helping the Sisters."

"I suppose I just find this stuff interesting. I'm not doing it to prepare for my retirement. And I don't want to live in the boondocks. So, give it a rest."

We rode in silence for several minutes, listening to the GPS directions. I must have missed a turn because I was being redirected. Betty was watching the countryside. I should have known her brain would still be cranking.

We hadn't been on the road too long before Betty asked if I knew anything about foundations. She was concerned about the Sisters sinking a lot of money into trying to run the B&B and restaurant so they could have resources to support themselves. If the nuns had a foundation, people could donate to support the charitable cause. Kind of like what Father Jim's foundation does to help people get on their feet.

I reminded Betty that a foundation had to have a mission. It couldn't just be a vehicle to employ people. And the mission had to focus on something educational or charitable. The B&B and restaurant didn't fit within that construct.

"We ought to research that," Betty said.

I nodded distractedly. The voice on the GPS announced that we had reached our destination. I turned into the lot and, given the heavy downpour, was pleased to find a parking spot not too far from the entrance.

"They probably have a public-use computer in here," I said as I retrieved our umbrellas and pocketbooks from the back seat. "You can find out about foundations while I work on the Smithfield's."

"I wouldn't know where to begin. I think you should do it. I'll just be your scribe."

"Whatever."

I sounded more like Amanda than myself with that last comment, but I was feeling a little annoyed. I wasn't sure why. Maybe I sensed Betty's detachment, and it was putting a damper on my enthusiasm.

I thought we could accomplish more with two of us doing research at the same time. That wasn't going to happen, so I'd best just get over my mood.

^^^

The receptionist at the historical society greeted us as we entered the spacious reading room. I explained the purpose of our visit and asked if there might be resources available to search for information about the Smithfield's. We were led to a reference area that had several computers, each set up on its own table with two chairs. Such an arrangement would work perfectly for Betty and me.

We were barely settled when a staff member arrived and introduced herself as Barbara. She told us that she'd be happy to gather any documents that might be pertinent to our search.

When I told Barbara about our quest, she mentioned that JW and Hildegarde had been respected residents of the county.

She thought we might want to read some of the old newspaper articles that had been archived and stored in a database for easy retrieval.

Barbara showed us how to locate those on the computer. She also pointed out photographs of the Smithfield's with some of their visiting dignitaries. For a small fee, we'd be permitted to make a copy of anything designated as printable.

Betty and I decided to start with the photos. I scrolled through pictures of the mansion during its construction and various views of the immature vineyard. We chose to print just two of those, then turned our attention to JW and Hildegarde.

Jonas Willard Smithfield was an imposing figure, a tall man dressed impeccably. In his younger years, he was clean-shaven, but had a moustache in later pictures. Hildegarde was slender, and much shorter than JW. Her blond hair was styled in a medium-length bob, characteristic of the day.

We printed pictures of the two of them standing on the lawn in front of the mansion, posing by what looked like a Model T automobile, and greeting various dignitaries. Betty wrote a short description on the reverse side of each print.

We then turned our attention to the newspaper articles. Several of the early ones highlighted the construction of the mansion, and included many of the archived photographs we had already reviewed.

The estate was apparently big news in the county, especially since the wealthy couple planned to reside there year-round. One editorial informed readers that this would benefit local farmers because of the tax revenue the Smithfield's would contribute. It also noted that other wealthy landowners were constructing summer homes, but those were located closer to the train line from the city.

Later articles documented that both JW and Hildegarde served on many prestigious boards and guilds, often donating goods and services. Hildegarde was admired, not only for her jams and jellies, but also for her involvement at the local hospital. She hosted fund-raising soirees to benefit families who couldn't afford medical care.

As I read the various articles aloud, Betty jotted notes that we could share with the Sisters. Barbara startled us when she appeared at the door saying, "I hate to disturb you, but we're closing in 15 minutes."

I glanced at my watch and saw that almost three hours had passed. I told Barbara that I needed to pay for the copies we had printed.

"That'll be fine," Barbara said. "I also thought you might want to take a look at this file about the vintage bowling alley in the Smithfield's basement. One of our staff writers had it on his desk. He's preparing to archive the information."

"Unless you'd let us stay a little longer, we won't have time to go through the file," I said with a glum expression.

"Unfortunately, we're not permitted to extend our hours. I can offer to make a copy for you since the information will be on our public website within the next few days. People are very interested in these old mansion bowling alleys."

"I'd appreciate that. We were hoping to learn more about its construction and the composition of the bowling balls."

"Do you think the Sisters would let our staff writer visit to take pictures of it?"

"I feel certain they would. Did you know that they turned part of the mansion into a B&B and restaurant?"

"No, I hadn't heard that."

"It would make an interesting story, don't you think?"

"I'll definitely mention it at a staff meeting. Whom should we call to set up a photo shoot?"

I gave Barbara the phone number for the monastery, and told her to ask for Sister Marian. We gathered our things and followed her to the reception desk where she quickly made a copy of the bowling alley file.

As I paid for the prints, I asked Barbara why there didn't seem to be any mention of investigations of the Smithfield's in the newspaper articles.

"What kind of investigations?" she asked.

"I'm not sure, but maybe about bootlegging."

"Why do you think there were investigations?"

"I did an internet search about JW the other day. There was some mention of it on one of the websites I visited."

"I wouldn't put much stock in that information," Barbara said. "Unless it came from a reputable site, the material could be bogus."

I agreed and we said our farewells. The rain had turned to a foggy mist as Betty and I departed. Barring any rush hour traffic, we planned to arrive back at the monastery in time for supper.

I was looking forward to hearing about the outcome of Leon's interview, and sharing what we had discovered in our search. The nuns were going to be really happy.

At least that's what I was thinking.

Chapter 26

Betty and I perused the dining room when we arrived at the monastery restaurant. I noticed that Father Jim and Leon were having dinner with Sister Marian. I thought it might be an indication that Leon would be staying. At least I was hoping so.

Cheryl and Cathy waved for us to join them, though they suggested that we stop at the steam table to fix our plates before we sat. Amanda had made a hearty beef stew, and there were slices of crusty bread and butter to accompany it.

"What's the story with Leon?" I asked, as I put my plate on the table. At the same time, Sister Cathy inquired about what information we had found at the historical society.

"You go first," I said. "I want to hear about Leon. Besides, Betty and I have a lot to tell you."

Cathy told us that they'd had a nice interview. The Sisters felt that Leon would work hard and support their mission. They could see that he wasn't always comfortable in new situations, but he gave a heartfelt explanation as to why he might be a good fit as groundskeeper.

"Leon will begin his employment on a trial basis for three weeks. If he doesn't feel that he's able to do the job, or his work is unacceptable, we'll part ways amicably."

"Will he stay in Charlie's cabin?" I asked.

"We all thought that would work well for Leon. Father Jim's going to stay in another poustinia for a few days to see how Leon adjusts."

"Joe might be able to show him some of the things he learned when he helped Charlie," I suggested.

"Definitely," Cheryl agreed. "And Marian's got a few ideas up her sleeves. Leon's going to be busy, that's for sure."

"Now tell us what you discovered about the Smithfield's today," Cathy pleaded.

"Very interesting information," I said as I handed Sister Cathy the file about the bowling alley, along with the copies of photographs. She flipped through the pages while Cheryl leaned over to view them with her.

Betty read through her notes, highlighting aspects of the news articles, and I interjected with further details. The four of us were really into it. Even Betty.

"The pictures are wonderful," Cathy said. "We saw some others in the boxes that Julie had found in the basement. It's nice to put faces on JW and Hildegarde."

"What else was in the boxes?" I asked.

"A bunch of recipes and some more ledgers. Most were very difficult to decipher."

"I'd like to see the recipes."

"You going to start cooking?" Betty asked.

"No, I want to see if there are instructions for making moonshine or some other kind of spirits."

"You really think JW was involved in bootlegging?"

"Yeah, I do. And I think the mechanism in the basement has something to do with it."

"I've always said you have quite an imagination," Betty declared as she buttered her bread.

"You can look through the recipes," Cathy said, chuckling at Betty's expression. "I didn't really notice what they were for. Most of them don't identify the final product."

"What's this file on the bowling alley?" Cheryl asked.

I explained that a staff member at the historical society was preparing to archive the information. "There's not a lot of detail, but it does indicate the type of wood used for the bowling alley's construction."

Cheryl scanned one of the documents in the file. "It says that most of the length of the lane was made of pine because of its durability. The pin deck and the first part of the lane where the bowler throws the ball was crafted from maple. Apparently, it has a much higher density and is able to absorb more shock."

I pointed to the section about the bowling balls. "Check this out. It says balls were made of *lignum vitae*, a tropical hard wood. I had no idea."

"We'll have fun reading through your notes and the file in the community room this evening," Cathy said. "I think it's cool to know more about the mansion's history."

"Barbara, the staff member at the historical society who helped us, is very interested in coming here to take pictures," I noted. "I gave Barbara the monastery's phone number, and told her to contact Sister Marian."

"We'll tell her. It might drum up more business for the B&B and restaurant."

"That's what I was thinking."

Sister Cathy asked if we found any intimation about JW's possible involvement in bootlegging in any of the newspaper articles. I told her there was not one iota. In fact, every news clip seemed a little too biased considering the historical aspects of the time. It made me wonder how JW was able to escape all of the scandals, intrigue, and corruption.

"Maybe the historical society archived only the positive articles," Cheryl said.

"That's possible," I agreed.

"Or maybe," Betty said, "JW was a decent guy who built a home in the country to escape the depravity of the times."

"We'll see," I said. "That's what I want to find out."

"The two of you sound like Julie and Dolores," Cheryl said. "I think you like to egg each other on."

"It's the sign of a strong friendship," I said with a wink to Betty. "Two old coots having a good time."

Chapter 27

I awoke at the crack of dawn on Friday morning. Although I attempted to turn over and grab another hour of sleep, my mind was a whirlwind of activity. I tried to picture myself dining with JW and Hildegarde, hobnobbing with prestigious dignitaries, posing for pictures on the front lawn. I wondered what the Smithfield's did all day besides serving on guilds and hosting benefits for the less fortunate. Did they take drives on the country roads? Did Hildegarde visit farm wife neighbors and share a cup of tea?

Knowing that my brain was too awake to hope for more sleep, I turned on the bedside light and shrugged off the covers. Before taking a quick shower, I heated water in the microwave and added a tea bag for it to steep while I dressed.

After making the bed, I carried my mug of tea to the cabin porch, pondering the mechanism in the monastery basement. I wanted to discover the reason for the click before I departed for home the next day.

I figured there had to be a secret compartment in one of the cupboards. Maybe even a hidden safe where JW had stashed millions of dollars from bootlegging. If we found it, the Sisters would be wealthy.

Father Jim startled me from my reverie as he called out a hearty "Good morning!"

"'Morning, Father. You out for your daily constitutional?'"

"Just coming back from Mass at the convent. You're up mighty early."

"Enjoying my last full day of peace and quiet. Would you like a cup of tea? It'll only take a minute to heat the water."

"Don't mind if I do," Father Jim said, as he sat on the other rocking chair. When I returned with his tea, I noticed that Father Jim seemed to be snoozing. He opened his eyes when I put the mug on the little table between us.

I'd say that Father Jim's probably in his late fifties. He's average height, not too muscular, and clean shaven. His gray hair made him look distinguished. I particularly liked the smile wrinkles around his sparkling blue eyes.

"What are your plans for the day?" he asked.

"I might do a little exploring. Looks like it's going to be a nice day, so I'll probably go to the lake after lunch."

"Amanda and Joe said you donated the new canoe. That was very generous of you."

"It was needed. Or so I'm told by our young friends."

Father Jim gave a hearty chuckle. "I hope to test it out this afternoon myself."

"You staying long?"

"Just a few days. I want to make sure Leon's OK. Besides, this place is a great getaway. I can totally relax."

"Me, too."

"Do you make it a retreat when you're here?" Father Jim asked, taking a sip of his tea.

"If you mean like a week of silence, no. I enjoy chatting with the nuns and Betty. But I don't have distractions like I do at home. You know, with TV and chores. I have time to ponder when I'm here."

"I know what you mean. I made a retreat here in early June. The poustinias are very conducive to solitude and prayer. But I also like to come just to re-energize my spirit."

"My neighbor thinks I'm crazy for spending my vacation in a rustic cabin."

"She'd have to experience it to know why you return. Amanda told me that she met you here last summer, and that you took her under your wing. She said you're close friends with her grandfather. I know she was quite upset when he moved to St. Louis."

"We were all surprised that he wanted to follow Sister Tony."

"Do you think he'll be back?"

"I have no idea. But it's not really my concern."

"Maybe I misunderstood Amanda. She seemed to think that the two of you were a couple."

"Just good friends."

I really didn't like the turn of this conversation, nor did I want to drag up something that I had done a good job of burying. I decided to change the subject by asking how he had become involved with the homeless shelter.

"I have no idea," Father Jim said with a chuckle. "It's one of those things in life that just seemed to unfold. You know what I mean?"

"I guess I do. That's kind of like how I found this place and the friendships that have been forged. So, you weren't assigned to work at the shelter?"

"No. As a young priest, I was assigned to a parish in the city. Over time, I realized that I needed to do more than tend to people's spiritual lives. Many folks were living hand to mouth. I asked the bishop if I could start a food pantry in the diocese."

"Obviously, he thought it was a good idea."

"Not at first. He was hesitant because there were other organizations in the city that provided such services. I was able to show him that more was needed, and he eventually gave his approval."

"And that grew into the shelter?"

"That grew into the soup kitchen. I got some volunteers to help me make soup from produce that we got from farmers' markets. If it was bruised or wilted, people didn't want it. But it was still nourishing. We learned how to feed a lot of families."

"Many people don't know how to make soup. They think it comes in a can."

"Exactly. At first we'd put the soup in plastic containers, and bring it to those who needed it. We outgrew my space in the rectory garage, so the bishop bought an old warehouse in the city and assigned me to be the director of the diocesan soup kitchen. I promised him I'd find a way for the place to become self-supporting."

"That couldn't have been easy since most of the patrons couldn't pay for a meal."

"You're right. I started speaking at parishes in the more affluent areas of the county, and accrued enough donations to start a foundation to fund the operation. Our place is big enough that we can now offer shelter, as well as a good meal."

"That's amazing!" I said. "Were you already a licensed counselor at that time?"

"Not at all. That was the next step. I asked the bishop if I could go on to study counseling psychology. I'm not sure if he understood the need or just wanted me out of his hair, but he gave his approval." We both laughed.

"He must be a pretty smart bishop."

"He's a great leader," Father Jim said. "He encourages us to find ways to deliver the gospel message, and he helps us to do that as best he can. There'd be no homeless shelter or soup kitchen in the city if it weren't for him."

"And you."

"I'm just the vehicle."

"Do you think Leon's going to work out here?" I asked.

"I don't know. I think it's the right environment, and I'm grateful that the Sisters are giving him a chance. Now he has to step up to the plate. And speaking about stepping, I need to meander over to his cabin to see if he's ready to get started."

"I enjoyed our chat."

"Me, too," Father Jim said as he took his leave. "Now stop burying your feelings about Charlie. Tell him that you miss him and want him to come home. Besides, this place needs a lot of work and the nuns can't do it all."

I refreshed my tea and did a little mulling about Father Jim's words. How'd he know that I had suppressed my feelings for Charlie? He must be very insightful, or I must be pretty darn transparent.

I thought about calling Charlie, but realized that he'd be working on a Friday morning. I decided to wait and give him a call tonight. In the meantime, I was hoping we'd find out what the mysterious click in the basement means.

Chapter 28

Sister Cathy and I had made arrangements to continue our exploration of the basement before lunch. When we met by the elevator, I told her that I was determined to identify the source of the click this very day. I shared my idea that the nodule in the floor might be the mechanism to open a hidden compartment, even a safe.

"That's what I was thinking, too," Cathy said. "But if it's a safe, why not put it in a handier place, like behind a picture on the main floor?"

"Maybe because that's the first place someone would look if planning a robbery. JW was apparently very smart. Guess that's how he got so rich."

We went straight to the gadget, getting on our hands and knees to examine it closely. It was a simple small, round button, totally unnoticeable since it was the exact color of the concrete floor.

We then checked the cabinet with the most pronounced sound of the click. That was simply a basic wardrobe, empty except for the metal pole to hang clothes. The pole appeared to be very sturdy, possibly a part of the original construction.

The ladder was where we had left it the other day. Sister Cathy continued her exploration of the top shelves, while I again went through all of the other cabinets. I knew they were empty except for the bowling balls and extra pin, but I wanted to check again.

I took out the smaller ball and examined it. "You know, it's really remarkable that these old balls were made of wood."

"We were reading about it in the file you got from the historical society," Cathy agreed. "They used a very heavy wood from the tropics."

I put my thumb and middle finger into the two holes and tossed the ball down the alley. Three pins went down.

"I wonder if the alley or the ball is warped," I said. "None of us has been able to get a strike."

"Wouldn't surprise me. The basement's a little damp."

I walked to the end of the alley to retrieve the ball and reset the pins. I carefully examined each pin. A few had begun to crack, but not significantly. They were still in pretty good shape.

I returned the ball to the cabinet, and examined the other ball and pin. Neither the ball nor the pin appeared damaged or misshapen. The pin, however, was different from the other pins set up on the alley.

"Hey, look at this," I said as I held the pin up to show Cathy. "It's got a hole in the bottom."

"Maybe termites got to it."

"No, I don't think so. Looks like it's been drilled."

I took it to the end of the alley to compare it with the other pins. None of them had a hole on the bottom.

On a whim, I put the extra pin over the button in the floor and it fit loosely. I pushed, but there was no click. I turned the pin full circle. Nothing. Removing the pin, I pushed on the nodule in the floor and heard the click.

"This is definitely weird," I said, looking perplexed. "This pin's made for something other than bowling. Maybe it's just a decoy."

Cathy came down from the ladder to take a look. She, too, fit the pin over the bump in the floor and nothing happened. I went back to the closet where we heard the click and searched for a raised nodule. The walls of the closet were smooth.

"How about under the pole?" Cathy asked.

"It looks like it's built in. I don't think it's removable."

"Can you turn it?"

I was able to turn the pole around in its sockets, but couldn't get the pole out of its brackets. Cathy wanted to try. She turned the pole towards her three or four times, and felt around the back of the brackets.

"I don't think the pole's built in," Cathy said. "It might be screwed in. The left bracket has a groove in the back of it."

She continued to turn the pole toward her, while pushing the left side of the pole to the back wall of the cabinet.

"Want me to push while you unscrew?" I asked.

"That might work," Cathy said. "Maybe it's rusted."

"Could be," I said, as I pushed with all of my strength. The left side of the pole popped out. Cathy continued to unscrew the right side, and the pole was freed from the cabinet.

"OK, now test the bowling pin on the screw that held the pole," Cathy said.

It fit perfectly. I turned the pin, but nothing happened.

"This is so frustrating," I said, trying to think of another option. "How about if I press the button in the floor, while you turn the bowling pin?"

We coordinated our movements. At the sound of the click, Cathy turned the pin towards her.

Still nothing. We both groaned, exasperated.

"Press it again," Cathy said with determination. "I'll turn the pin in the other direction."

Amazingly, the back of the closet began to slide to the left.

"Oh, my gosh," Cathy exclaimed. "It's a pocket door. And we've opened it!"

Excitedly, I rushed over to examine our find. It wasn't a hidden compartment or a safe. It was a passageway.

Cathy and I peered inside the doorway, but it was dark, and there were a lot of cobwebs. There was a musty odor from within.

"Oh, gross," Cathy said, scrunching her nose. "Good thing Cheryl didn't join us. She'd be screaming at the top of her lungs."

"We need a flashlight," I said. "I can't see if it leads to a room or what."

Cathy and I wanted to figure out how to close the pocket door before we went to get the nuns. She placed the bowling pin over the screw and turned the pin towards her. Sure enough, the door began to slide closed.

"That's absolutely amazing," I said.

Cheryl grinned. "It's just like a faucet. A sideways faucet. Righty tighty, lefty loosey."

Chapter 29

I t didn't take long for Cathy to find Sister Marian and Cheryl in the convent. I nabbed Dolores and Julie from the gift shop and told them of our find. Dolores handed me a battery lantern, then grabbed a few flashlights for good measure. We all met at the elevator.

"Did you tell Cheryl about the cobwebs?" I asked Cathy.

"She did," Cheryl said with a comical expression. "Believe me, I'm not going into any hole in the wall. I just want to see what you found."

Sister Cathy and I led the nuns to the wardrobe cabinet. She explained how we discovered that the extra bowling pin was a decoy, and that it was actually used to open the back of the closet.

"How in the world did you figure that out?" Julie asked.

"I have no idea," I said. "But it was like solving a puzzle. The pieces had to fit. In this case, the pin had to fit."

Cathy and I once again coordinated our movements. I pushed the button in the floor while she turned the pin towards the back wall of the closet. The pocket door slowly slid to the left.

"We need to call the police," Cheryl emphatically stated.

"Why?" We all seemed to answer at once.

"There could be a dead body in there. What if it's some kind of tomb?"

"It would stink like crazy," Dolores replied. "It's not a burial place. In fact, I detect a little movement of air."

"Close the door," Cheryl said, backing away. "There could be rats or something."

Julie piped up. "I want to check it out."

She took the lantern from me, placed it on the floor just beyond the pocket door frame, and peered in. The rest of us were gathered around the outer door of the wardrobe. Cheryl hung back, ready to bolt if she detected any peculiar movement from the tunnel.

"What do you see?" Marian asked.

"It's not a room," Julie replied. "I think it's some type of passageway. The light's not strong enough for me to see very far.

"Where's it lead to?" Dolores asked.

"How would I know?" Julie said as she joined the rest of us. "Why don't you go in and see."

"I'm not going in there. You think I'm crazy?"

I took Julie's place in the closet. Using the flashlight, I scanned the walls and floor just beyond the pocket door. Despite all of the cobwebs, I told the Sisters, the passage wasn't a rough dugout. In fact, the flooring was made of concrete, just like the basement. The walls and ceiling looked like some type of cinder block.

"Maybe it's a storm cellar," Marian said.

"I don't think so," I said, shaking my head, "Even with the flashlight and lantern, there's not enough light to see beyond a couple of feet. Besides, why go to such trouble to conceal the entrance?"

"Perhaps it was used to hide runaway slaves, like part of the Underground Railway," Dolores suggested.

"Probably not," Cheryl replied. "The mansion wasn't built until 1920 or so. Once the Civil War was over, there wasn't any need for the Underground Railway."

"Was there anything written about it in the boxes that Julie found?" I asked.

"I don't think so," Cathy stated. "Do you have any other boxes, Julie?"

"No. I only saved the ones that looked like they contained recipes. Probably a lot of stuff was trashed ages ago."

I offered to lead an expedition through the passage. No one else was interested. Even Cathy was reluctant, especially since we didn't know where it would lead us.

Sister Marian suggested that we close up everything and go to lunch. Amanda would be wondering where we were. Cheryl was more than ready to leave the basement. She said it gave her the creeps.

I was determined I'd be back to explore the tunnel.

Chapter 30

B etty and Amanda were having lunch together when we explorers arrived at the dining room. The two of them were engaged in conversation, but welcomed us with a questioning gaze. Amanda seemed a little miffed that she hadn't been included in any adventure we might have experienced.

"Where've you guys been?" Amanda asked, somewhat petulantly.

"Vicki and Sister Cathy found a secret passageway in the basement," Marian said.

"No way!" Amanda exclaimed. "Where?"

"In the closet with the click," Cheryl said. "Don't worry. We'll tell you all about it. But it's disgusting down there. I'm going to wash up. I feel like I have creepy crawlers on me."

I made a sandwich at the sideboard, then joined Betty and Amanda. The Sisters fixed their plates, and sat at two other tables.

"So, tell us about it," Amanda said, barely waiting for me to spread my napkin across my lap.

I explained how the extra bowling pin was the key to solving the riddle. I made sure to add plenty of details with appropriate pauses to extend the narrative and, as usual, drive Amanda crazy.

"Geez," she said. "Joe's going to want to see it as soon as he gets back from the diner." She excused herself to go to the kitchen and call him.

Betty and I chuckled at Amanda's sudden departure. We both agreed that Joe had become a priority in Amanda's life. It wasn't a negative thing. The two of them made a great couple. I just wondered if Amanda was ready for a serious relationship.

"Sounds like you solved your mystery," Betty noted after refreshing her iced tea.

"You know the old saying that if one door closes, another one opens?" I asked.

"Yeah."

"Well, now we have a new mystery to solve. Where will the hidden door take us?"

"You're a piece of work!"

"So you've told me. Bottom line is, I don't want to leave until I figure it out."

"Seems to me you're out of luck. The place is booked solid this weekend. Remember?"

"I know. Maybe I'll bunk in Amanda's room."

"Kate will be here. It's Friday."

"Help me figure out how I can extend my stay."

"Thought you didn't like the boondocks."

"I'm serious, Betty. I want to discover where the passage leads."

"Find a map. You'd be nuts to go through a tunnel before it's examined by an engineer. It could collapse."

I told Betty that the passage looked pretty solid to me. Besides, we didn't find any sort of blueprint. She suggested that I check it out above ground, estimating where the tunnel might lead.

I wasn't convinced that would work. We didn't know if there were twists and turns underground, nor the length of the passageway.

"Start with a straight line, and see where that takes you."

"Probably to the parking lot," I said.

"See? It's a lost cause," Betty said. "Whatever was there is now long gone."

"Unless the tunnel goes beyond where the lot's located."

"Pretty thick woods back there."

"I know. You want to explore with me this afternoon?"

"No, I want to go to the lake."

"Please? We could just take a little walk. We'll still have time to hit the beach."

"Sometimes you drive me crazy."

"I know."

"All right. I'll go. But if I see poison ivy or any critters, I'm out of there."

"It's a deal," I said.

^^^

Betty insisted that we inform the Sisters where we planned to investigate as we left the dining room. I figured it was better to be safe than sorry.

We met Father Jim and Leon in the hallway as we were leaving. Leon was pretty sweaty, so he excused himself to wash up in the men's room.

"Doing any exploring?" Father Jim asked me.

"As we speak," I said.

"She found a secret passageway in the basement," Betty said. "Now we have to figure out where it leads. We're headed to the woods." She rolled her eyes.

"Why don't you just go through the passage?" Father Jim asked.

"Betty thinks it's too dangerous."

"Probably true."

"Go eat lunch," I said when Leon returned. "The nuns can tell you all about it."

"You want Leon to go with you?"

"Not right now. The poor guy looks like he needs a good meal."

"Yes, ma'am," Leon said. "But I can help you if you want."

"Maybe later," I said. "Thanks, Leon. We're just going to take a quick look, then we're going to the lake."

"We're going there after lunch as well," Father Jim noted. "Leon wants to see if he can devise some type of shelter for the canoes. We'll catch up with you then."

As we left the building, I estimated where the doorway to the passage was from the outside of the mansion. A straight line took us across the lawn, across the driveway, and across the parking lot. As we got to the far edge of the parking lot, I looked back to gauge if we were still in a direct line.

Betty peered into the woods. "I don't think I want to go in there. There's not even a path."

"Where's your sense of adventure?" I asked as I pushed aside a thicket of brambles.

Betty didn't respond, but she did follow me. After we had gone about 30 feet, I turned and said, "This is a lost cause."

"Thank goodness you've come to your senses."

"We need a machete or something to clear an opening. Besides, it'd be easy to get turned around and totally lost."

"I agree. Let's get out of here."

We made our way back to the parking lot. I could see that we both had numerous scratches from the vines.

"I guess that wasn't such a smart idea," I said as I wiped a drop of blood off my arm.

"You've had better ones," Betty muttered.

"You're the one who came up with this brainstorm."

"I said to look at a map. I didn't expect to risk life and limb in a jungle."

"We're going to have to go through the tunnel," I said.

"Speak for yourself, kemosabe."

We turned to walk toward our cabins. Mulling out loud, I told Betty that the only way to solve the mystery would be to explore the tunnel, especially since we couldn't locate anything from the outside.

I'd have to find someone to accompany me, and I knew it wouldn't be Betty. There was no doubt in my mind that JW was selling illegal spirits. I was certain that the secret door was going to lead me to the site of his enterprise.

"What makes you so sure?" Betty asked.

"Think about it. The Smithfield's lived during the time of prohibition. They were wealthy. They had a vineyard. They kept cryptic ledgers. They had a hidden passage."

"So what if they did? Why do you care?"

"I don't know. I guess I want to solve the mystery."

"Let's give it a rest for a while," Betty said as we reached my cabin. "I'm going to take a shower, then I'm going to the lake for one last afternoon of peace."

Chapter 31

By the time I got to the lake, Betty was already spread out on her towel. She appeared to be dozing, but opened one eye as I put my gear on the beach and sat down. I told her how much I appreciated that she had come with me into the woods. Betty sat up, donning her hat to shield her eyes from the bright sunlight.

"It's a good thing we're friends," she replied. "I told you before. I think it's all a wild goose chase."

"Probably. Do you want to try out the new canoe?"

We dragged the canoe into the lake. Betty held it steady until I got settled, then she hopped in. We paddled toward the raft, then let the canoe drift while we rested our arms.

An egret landing on the beach at the far side of the lake caught my attention. I watched as it softly glided to firm ground.

Betty followed my gaze before speaking. "When we took the boys camping, John always told them that seeing an egret was a sign of good luck."

"In what way?"

"I guess in the eye of the beholder. For me, I always felt that I was lucky to be loved by such a remarkable man."

"I wish I could have met him."

"The two of you would have really hit it off. John loved solving a good mystery."

"Did the boys fall for the lucky egret line?"

"They sure did. After a sighting, they'd tell stories around the campfire about the luck they'd had that day. Could've been catching a fish or finding a special rock." Betty chuckled at the memory. "And, of course, John would egg them on with some wild tale about his own good fortune."

"That's funny. Maybe I'll have luck solving the mystery of the mansion. I'll bet there's a still—or the remnants of one—somewhere on the property."

"You never know," Betty said, humoring me.

By the time we beached the canoe, we saw that Father Jim and Leon had arrived. Before we could warn him, Leon took a running leap into the frigid lake and came up gasping. We all had a good laugh. Once his body adjusted to the cold water, he began to swim to the anchored raft.

Father Jim spread his towel next to ours, and asked if we had found anything in the woods. I told him we didn't get too far because of all the brambles. Betty showed him her wounds for good measure.

"What are you looking for?"

"Vicki thinks the tunnel leads to a still. She's trying to find it," Betty said.

"Seems a bit far-fetched, but not entirely unreasonable."

Encouraged by the smallest validation, I proceeded to tell Father Jim details of my research about the early days of the mansion. I thought my summary provided a good rationale for finding evidence of some type of alcoholic beverage production connected with our discovery.

I ended my speech by saying that I hoped Joe would want to explore the tunnel with me when he got back from work at the diner. Betty and Father Jim disagreed, reminding me that Friday nights were hectic, especially when the place was booked solid for the weekend.

I was about to respond when Leon returned from his swim. Father Jim handed Leon his towel, and motioned for him to join us. "Guess it was a tad chilly," Father Jim teased.

"Just about froze my... Oops, sorry ladies." We all had a good chuckle.

"How was your first night in a poustinia?" I asked Leon.

"Pretty nice, ma'am. Felt kind of strange, but good."

I told him about my first night, and how a storm had frightened me. "That's how I met Amanda," I said.

"Yes, ma'am. She told me about it."

"You don't have to call me ma'am," I said. "Please call me Vicki."

"I been taught to call ladies ma'am, ma'am. I'm a soldier. But I'll try to remember to call you Vicki."

"I heard you started working here today," I said.

"Yes, ma'am. I mean Vicki. Cut the back field for Sister Marian. After I cool off a bit, I'm going to weed the gardens by the monastery. She told me to take a break."

"When you moved the tractor out of the garage, did you happen to see anything like a backhoe?" I asked.

"No, ma'am. Nothing like that."

Betty explained to Leon that I thought the hidden tunnel in the basement was an indication that the original owners of the mansion were bootlegging. "Now she wants to chop down trees beyond the parking lot to find some imaginary still."

"I can clear the woods for you, ma'am," Leon said.

"Not unless Sister Marian asks you," Father Jim reminded him. "Sister Marian's the boss. We talked about this."

"Yes, sir. I remember."

"Sounds like good advice," I agreed. "Between the Sisters and the guests, lots of people could be asking you to do things for them. Better to follow only one leader."

"Yes, ma'am, Miss Vicki. But I'll ask the boss if she wants me to clear out that part of the property."

"Thank you, Leon. That would be wonderful."

"Aren't you leaving tomorrow?" Father Jim asked.

"Uh oh. Sore subject, Father," Betty said.

"I'm going to ask Julie if there's anything available next weekend. Now that I think about it, my neighbor, Myra, said she'd like to come for a couple of days."

"Isn't that Kate's grandmother?" Father Jim asked.

"Yeah. It'd be nice if she can come when Kate's here."

"Who's going to watch your dog?"

"I haven't figured that out yet."

"I can do it," Leon said. "He can follow me around when I'm working. Maybe even stay in my cabin."

"Harvey would like that, Leon. Thank you. Sister Tony didn't permit guests to bring animals. I'll have to ask Sister Julie since she's now in charge of reservations."

"You guys can work it out," Betty said while she shook the sand from her towel. "I'm going to get out of this sun and take a nap."

I decided to bid my leave also. Sister Julie would be busy with the weekend guests arriving if I waited too long before asking about bringing Harvey. Besides, I'd have to call Myra first. She might not even be interested in a weekend getaway on such short notice.

While I gathered my stuff, Betty and I made plans to meet for supper at the restaurant. Leon and Father Jim added that they'd be there as well.

"Now's your chance to test the new canoe," Betty called over her shoulder.

"Just what we were thinking. Catch you later."

Chapter 32

When I got back to my cabin, I took a quick shower and dressed for dinner before calling Myra. It gave me time to plan how I might convince her to come with me to the monastery next weekend. I wasn't sure why it was so important to me. Perhaps it was as simple as wanting to share my experience. It would give Myra a better understanding about the place.

I grabbed my phone and novel, opting to enjoy the fresh air on the front porch. Myra answered on the second ring. She was rather surprised to hear from me, perhaps half expecting that I'd decided to stay another week. We chatted about Harvey before I told her my plans.

"That boy sure makes himself comfy," Myra said with a giggle. "You should see how he sprawls out on the sofa. Barely have room to sit and watch my shows."

"Tell Harvey to get down. He can lie on the floor."

"I don't mind. He's good company. You coming home tomorrow?"

"I am. Probably sometime late afternoon. I want to do a little more exploring in the morning."

"What are you looking for?"

"A still. I'll tell you all about it tomorrow."

"The nuns need a still? I thought they sent their grapes out for production."

"They do. It's not for the Sisters. I'm looking for one built by the original owners."

"You sure do get yourself involved out there."

"I'm having so much fun that I want to come back next weekend. You want to join me? Kate should be here."

"I'd enjoy seeing the place. But what about Harvey?"

"I'm going to ask Sister Julie if I'd be allowed to bring him. Leon, the new groundskeeper, said he'd watch him."

Myra reminded me that she didn't want to stay in a cabin. I told her that I was planning to book two rooms in the B&B, but wanted to check with her first. Surprisingly, she agreed readily.

After insisting that I make my own reservation first, with whatever's available, Myra said she'd leave her options open. If the B&B was full, she'd watch Harvey so I could do my sleuthing. That's just how she is.

When our conversation was finished, I called Sister Julie. After making dinner reservations for the evening, I asked about the availability of rooms in the B&B next weekend.

"You're going for the comfortable quarters?"

"Kate's grandmother would like to visit. She doesn't want to stay in a poustinia, so I figured we might each be able to get a room in the B&B."

"You're in luck," Julie said within a few minutes. "I'll add you both to the register."

"That's great. My only dilemma is that Myra takes care of my dog when I go away. Do you think I'd be permitted to bring him? Leon said that Harvey could stay in his cabin."

"I don't know about that. I'll have to check with Sister Marian."

"I understand. I know Sister Tony didn't permit animals, but this is a special circumstance. I'd really like Myra to see the place."

"Marian loves dogs, so she might agree," Julie said. "I'll let you know when I see you later. Did you and Betty find anything in the woods?"

"No. There's no path and too many trees and brambles. We didn't make it very far."

"I don't think we've ever cleared out that section beyond the parking lot," Julie said. "When we put in the lot, that whole area was deeply wooded."

"Do you remember if they found anything of interest when they cleared the land?"

"Not a thing. I know we sold the trees to some lumber company, and we had a bonfire with the brush. No, nothing of interest."

"So the tunnel couldn't have ended there."

"If it did, there was no exit above ground."

"That's got to be one long tunnel."

"Maybe it's not a tunnel. It could be just a passageway to a storage room. You know, like a wine cellar or something."

"But why hide the entrance?"

"Prohibition?"

"I guess that's possible. I'd like to check it out tomorrow morning before I leave."

"I think Cathy's planning to explore after Mass. I heard her talking to Joe about it when he came in this afternoon."

After our conversation, I tried to read, but my thoughts kept returning to the purpose of the mansion's hidden portal. If the tunnel led to a storeroom as Julie suggested, why did JW go to the trouble of making it inaccessible? And, unless there was another mechanism that we hadn't yet found, two people were needed to open the door.

None of it made any sense to me. Julie was correct about the era of prohibition being one of secrecy and distrust. And the mansion was built during that timeframe. The ledger fueled my belief that the Smithfield's were doing something illegal.

Reflecting on my involvement, I felt certain that solving the mystery would add historical value to the Monastery of St. Carmella. If anything, the publicity might draw more visitors to the B&B and restaurant.

Chapter 33

Sister Cathy, Joe, and I met at the monastery entrance on Saturday morning, each of us carrying flashlights. I had already checked out of my poustinia, and loaded my bags in the car. Betty had departed after breakfast. Cathy told us that she put a couple of lanterns and two brooms in the basement before Mass.

The three of us made our way to the bowling alley. Cathy and I showed Joe how we had found the hidden doorway. We removed the clothes pole from the built-in wardrobe, then I stationed myself at the nodule in the floor. When Cathy had the decoy pin in place, she gave me the signal to coordinate our movements. It was something schmaltzy like "abracadabra." Joe gazed in awe as the back wall slid open.

"This is amazing," Joe said, beaming his flashlight into the opening. He brushed away a cobweb, and took a step forward. Cathy handed him a lantern which he placed on the tunnel floor. I set the additional lantern in the closet for extra light.

Joe advanced slowly, seeming to disregard Sister Cathy's warning about not going too far. As Joe's eyes adjusted to the dimness, he gave a whoop of excitement. Suddenly the tunnel was illuminated with a soft glow.

"How'd you do that?" I asked as I took a closer look.

"I pulled the little chain on the light fixture not too far from the entrance," Joe said. "Geez, the tunnel must be wired for electricity."

Sure enough, there was a simple sconce on the wall with a single bulb. A short chain was the light's switch. The tunnel looked to be at least 3 feet wide and about 6 feet in height. Some type of concrete blocks lined the walls and roof, while poured concrete made the floor solid and smooth. It was obvious that, once again, JW had spared no expense.

Joe moved forward while Cathy and I followed gingerly behind him. He switched on light fixtures as he proceeded. They were positioned about every 20 feet or so, although a few bulbs no longer worked.

Sister Cathy paused occasionally to sweep down a large cobweb or a daddy longlegs. I wasn't too worried about those critters, but I kept my eyes open for any potentially venomous spiders.

I looked back to gauge our distance and estimated that we had traveled in a straight line and were now probably under the parking lot. We walked another 100 feet or so, when I heard Joe say, "Uh oh."

"What's the matter?" Cathy asked.

"There's a closed door. And no door knob."

When we caught up to him, Joe was feeling all around the door frame, looking for some way to open it. I offered to go back to get the decoy bowling pin, but Joe thought that didn't make sense. Why would anyone want to carry it all the way through the tunnel?

"JW apparently liked pocket doors," Cathy said. "Look for some kind of button, then see if you can slide the door to the right or left."

"I found it!" Joe exclaimed.

The three of us were enveloped in dim daylight when we stepped into the cavernous structure. We each gazed around the room. My insides churned with excitement.

"Looks like you were right," Cathy said to me. Her voice had a tone of awe.

"Oh, my gosh," I said, practically in a whisper. There were several stalls to the left of us. Three of them were full of barrels. The fourth one housed the still.

The apparatus for the still used an oak barrel as the base. Copper tubing spiraled into a copper cask that was positioned over a makeshift stove. The heater, possibly fueled by kerosene, was vented through the concrete side wall. An empty glass jug was placed on the floor under a spigot located at the bottom of the barrel.

To the right of us was a ramp leading to the upper level. Joe located the button for opening the pocket door at the top of the incline. The three of us peered into a ramshackle wooden shed. An old hay wagon that had seen better days was near the doorway. Part of the roof of the structure had given way, while ivy and brambles protruded into the frame's rotted slats.

Joe took out his cell phone and began taking pictures. He muttered, "No one's going to believe this."

We headed back to the mansion, taking the time to close doors and switch off lights as we went. Joe took one last picture, a selfie, with the three of us in front of the wardrobe that had hidden the secrets of JW and Hildegarde Smithfield.

^^^

Amanda was not very happy when we got to the dining room. In fact, it appeared that she was ready to come looking for us. She complained that Joe was supposed to relieve her a half hour ago. Instead, Kate was trying to manage the kitchen alone.

"You're not going to believe what we found," Joe said in a soft tone.

"Why are you whispering?"

"Because I don't want any guests to hear about it. So keep quiet."

"You're covered with spider webs. Gross. You'd better go clean up before you prepare any food."

"I will, but we have to find Sister Marian."

"She's at the far table having lunch with Father Jim and Leon."

Marian glanced up from her conversation as the three of us approached. Amanda followed, curiosity getting the better of her. Once again Joe said, "You're not going to believe what we found." Father Jim pulled over some chairs from the next table.

"Spiders?" Marian said with a chuckle.

"Vicki was right," Cathy said. "JW was a bootlegger. We found the still."

"You've got to be kidding."

"Honest to goodness. It's no wonder investigators never found anything of interest. JW went to a great deal of trouble to keep his business hidden. Given the number of barrels we found, the Smithfield's had quite a profitable enterprise."

Joe showed the pictures he had taken to Marian, then to Father Jim and Leon. Each of them made a comment about our amazing find.

"Where's this room with the barrels located?" Marian asked.

"Exactly where Betty and I explored yesterday," I said. "It's only about 100 feet beyond the parking lot, but the woods are so overgrown there that no one would be able to find it."

"Leon mentioned that he'd be willing to clear out that area of our land, but I'm not too sure it would be the wise thing to do now," Marian said.

"No, ma'am. You might need to contact authorities or something."

"Why?" Amanda asked. "The nuns haven't done anything wrong."

"Of course not," Father Jim said. "But JW's still is going to put this place on the national historic register."

"You should call the county historical society," I said with gusto. "They'll know what to do."

"Interestingly, I got a call from them yesterday," Marian replied. "Couldn't be better timing. They're coming on Monday to take pictures of the bowling alley."

"Wait 'til they see what we found," Amanda said with an excited giggle.

"We?" Joe questioned while he put his cell phone in his pocket.

"OK. What you guys found," Amanda said. "But I would've been there if I hadn't had to prepare lunch."

"You can be with us for the photo shoot," Marian said. "In fact, maybe Joe can show you everything after lunch, and you can be the tour guide for the folks from the historical society."

"Awesome. That'll work."

Cathy told us she was going to take a shower and would be back to help clean up after lunch service. Joe said that he'd do the same and return shortly to work in the kitchen. Amanda just looked exasperated, reminding Joe to hurry.

Marian invited me to join her table for lunch. I begged off, saying that I didn't want to overstay my welcome. She wouldn't take no for an answer. Besides, she wanted to hear more about JW and our remarkable discovery.

Chapter 34

I could barely contain my elation when I arrived at Myra's house to pick up Harvey. She invited me to stay for a cup of tea, and Harvey welcomed me enthusiastically. I sat at the kitchen table while Myra put on the kettle, and I told her about our discovery of the Smithfield's still. I didn't leave out a single detail.

"How about that?" Myra said with a broad smile when she handed me a steaming mug, and put a plate of homemade cookies on the table. "The nuns inherited a bootleg operation. That's kind of funny."

"I hadn't thought about it like that, but I guess it is," I said with a chuckle. "I just think it's amazing to find a piece of history in a place you'd never expect."

"How do the Sisters feel about it?"

"They're still astonished. I mean, really. They've lived in the place for almost 70 years and had no idea."

"Surely the early nuns found some documentation when they first moved in, don't you think?"

"Anything they found was cryptic. As a novice, Sister Julie salvaged a couple of cartons when they were cleaning out the basement. She forgot all about them until Sister Cathy and I were looking for old papers."

"What was in the boxes?"

"Ledgers and recipes. Nothing to lead them to suspect that their home had a hidden passageway and was the site of illegal activity."

Harvey nudged me, no doubt begging for a piece of my cookie. Instead, I rubbed his head and told him how much I'd missed him.

Myra handed me a treat for Harvey, before asking why Sister Cathy and I had been searching for things in the mansion basement. Harvey wolfed the biscuit, then settled himself under my chair.

I told Myra how the Sisters and I had been talking about the original owners of the mansion. None of the Sisters knew too much about JW and Hildegarde Smithfield. Only that they were childless and had servants. Cathy and I just wanted to find out more about them.

"Looks like you uncovered a rat's nest," Myra said.

"I know. It's pretty amazing because the county records indicated that the Smithfield's were highly regarded. I'm reeling, just thinking about it."

"Now I *really* want to see the place."

"You will. This weekend. We're both staying in the B&B, and Harvey can come. He'll stay in Leon's cabin." Harvey's tail thumped on the kitchen floor when he heard his name.

"Who's Leon?"

"He's the new groundskeeper. Nice guy."

"You like him as much as Charlie?"

"I like him. Just not the same way."

"Maybe because you're in love with Charlie?"

"Give it a rest, Myra. Charlie's gone."

I gave Myra one of my looks. She knew it was time to change the subject.

"Does Kate know that I'll be there on the weekend?"

"I told her. She's really happy about it. Wants to show you all around."

"Yeah, but she's going to be working."

"She gets some breaks. Besides, I can fill in for her. You know, maybe do a little prepping or waitressing."

Myra was laughing when I put my cup in the sink.

"What's so funny?" I asked.

"I can't wait to see you as a waitress!"

^^^

After supper, I called Betty to tell her about our discovery of the still. She had lots of questions. Where was it? How did we find it? That kind of stuff. Despite Betty's usual lack of interest in the subject, she seemed pretty excited.

"Wait 'til the historical society hears about this," she said.

"I know. They're going to take pictures of the bowling alley on Monday. Marian told Amanda that she could give them a tour of the hidden passage."

"Once the newspapers get wind of it, the Sisters won't know what hit them."

We chatted about the potential of free publicity for the B&B and restaurant. Despite the fact that the monastery had once been a site of illegal activity, it wouldn't be attributed to the nuns. But it could certainly attract curious visitors.

Betty suggested that we reserve a poustinia right away if we want any chance of returning at the end of August. I hadn't even thought about that.

I told Betty that I also wanted to be there for the harvest of the grapes. We had done that last year and, though it was hard work, it was a very special time for me. "It'll seem strange this year without Charlie and Sister Tony orchestrating the harvest, but I still want to be a part of it."

We both checked our calendars and picked a date. Betty promised to call Sister Julie to make our reservations as soon as we ended the call.

"Did you call Charlie to tell him about your find?" Betty asked.

"No. Maybe I'll talk to him later. Besides, I'm sure Marian called Tony. She'll tell him."

"I imagine he'd like to hear it from you."

Betty wouldn't let me go until I promised to call him. Double cross my heart promise.

^^^

Charlie and I had a good chat. He said he knew exactly the area that I referred to when I told him where we found the still. He had wanted to clear that section, more as a safety feature for the parking lot, but never got around to it. Just didn't seem to be a priority.

I asked Charlie if he was adjusting to his new location. Although I recognized that it takes time to adapt to a move, I was surprised that he admitted he didn't like it there. If my memory served me, I had told him he wouldn't enjoy living in the city. No use rubbing his nose in it. I reminded him that he could always come back to the monastery.

"That's what Amanda told me, but it wouldn't be right."

"Why not? The Sisters said you'd always have a home at the monastery."

"The new guy's living in my cabin."

"He might not work out," I said.

"Doesn't matter. I heard that he'd been a homeless vet. I've been homeless. He needs a fighting chance."

I knew there was no use belaboring my point. Charlie's as stubborn as he is quiet. He'd dig in his heels and block further discussion. Amanda must have inherited his tenacity.

As Myra often reminded me, I'd have to use psychology. I changed the subject, telling Charlie about purchasing the new canoe.

"Amanda mentioned it to me. Said you donated it."

"Did she tell you it was her idea?"

"That girl's a piece of work," Charlie said with a chuckle. "Don't know where she gets it from."

"She's doing fine with the restaurant, you know," I said. "I'm really impressed with all that she's accomplished."

"Me, too. Think she'll ever hook up with Joe?"

"I haven't asked her, but they're becoming quite a couple. I kind of feel sorry for Kate."

"Is she upset about it?"

"Doesn't seem so, but she's always a third wheel. I think Sister Cheryl has taken Kate under her wing. Cheryl helps out a lot in the kitchen."

"Kate's still friends with Amanda, isn't she?"

"Oh, yeah. They're fine. Just that if Joe's around, Amanda only has eyes for him."

Charlie laughed. "Guess that's how it's supposed to be."

We chatted awhile longer, which surprised me because Charlie's not very long-winded. I had to admit, it had been a fine ending for a most remarkable day.

Chapter 35

I was able to wrap up things at work a little early on Friday. I loaded my car with a small suitcase and all of the stuff that Harvey would need for a weekend in the country. Myra was ready when I picked her up just before 4 p.m. We planned on arriving at the monastery in time for supper.

Myra seemed excited about her outing, and we chatted during the entire trip. Leon was waiting for our arrival at the monastery. He was kind enough to put Harvey on the leash and told us that he'd walk him to his cabin while we got settled. I gave Leon the bag of food and treats and Myra added her two cents about Harvey's likes and dislikes. Harvey was quite happy to explore this new territory.

After we checked in, Sister Julie showed us to our rooms. I thought it was sweet of her to put Myra next to Amanda's room. That's where Kate stayed on weekends. I was put directly across from them. Myra dropped her belongings on the bed, then gazed at the view from her window. Voicing her approval, she checked my accommodations as well.

Myra and I freshened up, then took the elevator to the dining room. Sister Julie must have told Kate that we had arrived because she was waiting at the entrance of the restaurant.

"I'm so happy you've come for the weekend," Kate said, giving her grandmother a kiss. "You're going to love this place."

"I can already see why you like it here. It's lovely. Now, you don't need to worry about me this evening. Vicki and I plan to have supper, then Sister Julie promised to take us for a little ride in her golf cart."

"That's great. Tell her to show you the lake."

"I sure will. Where would you like us to sit?"

Kate took us to a table set for two near one of the large windows overlooking the garden. I introduced Myra to several of the Sisters as we passed their table.

"They seem very nice," Myra whispered to me as I helped push in her chair. "But they don't look like nuns."

"You're thinking of the old days," I said with a chuckle. "Actually, some of the Sisters in the infirmary still wear a habit, but the younger ones wear regular clothes."

Kate returned with two glasses of ice water and handed each of us a menu. She also recited the specials being offered. When I mentioned that it didn't look too hectic this evening, Kate explained that some of the Sisters and Leon ate earlier. Most of the B&B guests hadn't yet checked in. She figured they'd probably be busy all day tomorrow.

"I want you to have time with your grandmother this weekend," I said, "so, I'll be happy to relieve you."

"Nonsense," Myra said. "What would Kate and I do? Sit in the parlor like two old ladies? Just give Vicki and me a job in the kitchen when you're there, Kate. We can have plenty of fun chopping vegetables or something."

"Joe already told me that he'd like you to make a few of your pies," Kate said. "He wants to learn your trick for a flaky crust."

"That's a deal. Now what do you recommend that I order for supper?"

Kate made a few suggestions. In the end, Myra and I both selected the seafood combo. As we waited for our food to arrive, we each had a warm crusty roll with butter.

Myra checked out the dining room and commented on its attractive décor. "This looks like a real restaurant. I mean, look, it's even got a cash register and all."

"It wasn't hard to transform it. You know Amanda's got a knack for decorating." I added in a whisper, "Ask what she did with the picture of the Last Supper."

"I can only imagine," Myra said with a chuckle.

When Kate returned with our entrees, she told us that Sister Cheryl and she would be joining us for dessert. Myra was concerned that Kate might get in trouble for sitting on the job, but Kate insisted that it was Cheryl's idea. "Besides, I can keep an eye on my tables. I really want you to meet Cheryl.

I explained that Sister Cheryl was ultimately in charge of the restaurant. She oversaw the operations and gave the chefs a break when she could. She also often helped with the prepping and clean-up.

Myra commented that she must be a wise woman. That type of leadership keeps everyone from getting burned out. Kate and I both agreed before she left to welcome a couple who had just arrived.

When Kate was out of earshot, I remarked in a low tone, "I have to admit, the new Sisters have added a dimension to the monastery that I wouldn't have thought possible. Don't get me wrong. Sister Tony had great vision, but I don't know that she'd have had the stamina to do all of this herself."

"I remember when you were upset that she was leaving," Myra noted, wrapping linguini around her fork. "Seems to me you said something about the new head nun being wet behind the ears."

I laughed and said, "Live and learn. Sister Marian's really great, as are her friends. You'll have a chance to get to know them this weekend."

"I hope they'll let you show me the tunnel you found."

"We can ask Marian or Cathy. Cheryl's not as interested. She's afraid of spiders."

"Maybe they spiffed it up to get ready for the photo shoot. How'd that go?"

"Amanda told me that the folks at the historical society were absolutely amazed. They took lots of pictures and said they hoped that the barn with the still will be restored."

We were still talking about the secret passage when Kate returned to take our dessert orders. As she cleared our plates, we informed her that we'd both like the mousse. In no time at all, Kate and Cheryl arrived at the table with the desserts. Kate introduced Myra to Sister Cheryl.

"I hear you're Kate's boss," Myra said.

"I guess I am, technically. But I'm still learning the ropes."

"Do you have a culinary degree?"

"No. I'm a teacher. But now the roles are reversed. Kate, Amanda, and Joe are teaching me."

"Don't be so modest," Kate said. "I'm learning a lot from you. Like how to stay calm when things get crazy around here."

Cheryl laughed. "It does get hectic, for sure. Especially on a weekend."

"Wait 'til the place gets on the national historic register," I said with a wry smile.

"Don't even remind me," Cheryl replied, rolling her eyes. "I mean it's great in some ways, but I'm not sure we're ready for all the publicity. And we certainly don't want it to impact our spiritual lives."

"How do you even have time to pray?" Myra asked.

"That's our priority, of course. I get up early for an hour of meditation, then we have Morning Prayer together, followed by Mass. I try to do some spiritual reading in the late afternoon, then we have Vespers before dinner."

"The nuns let me go to Vespers when I'm here," Kate said.

"What are Vespers?" Myra asked.

"It's a bunch of prayers like psalms and stuff," Kate said. "We take turns reading the passages out loud. It's cool."

"When did you get so interested in religion?" Myra asked.

"I don't know. Guess I started to go to Mass on Sundays because I liked hearing Father Jim preach. Then Cheryl invited me to Vespers. I think it's really neat, though Amanda thinks I'm being kooky. Anyway, that's what she told me."

"We're going to miss Kate when she starts college in the fall," Cheryl said.

"Don't worry. I'll be back whenever I can."

"Gosh," I said. "What *are* you going to do when Kate goes back to school? I hadn't thought about that."

"Guess we'll have to hire part-time help. That'll be a pain in the neck. I hate interviewing."

My ears picked up. "That's what I love to do!"

"Good," Cheryl said. "You can mentor me. Or maybe I'll save the interviews for the weekends you come to visit."

By the time we finished our desserts, a few new guests had arrived. Kate excused herself to show them to their tables. Cheryl offered to check us out at the register. She processed our credit cards, reminding us that Sister Julie was in the gift shop waiting to take us on a tour.

"I've so enjoyed meeting you," Myra said to Cheryl.

"Likewise," Cheryl replied with her engaging smile. "I'll see you in the morning. Coffee and tea are available beginning at 6 a.m. Breakfast service starts at 8:30.

^^^

Julie was an excellent tour guide, and Myra was quite impressed with the vineyard and lake. We made a stop at Leon's cabin so I could check on Harvey. Leon was resting on his porch with Harvey snoozing at his feet. He opened an eye and wagged his tail when he saw us approaching.

"I thought for sure he'd be chasing squirrels," I said to Leon.

"Yes, ma'am. He's been doing that. I'd say he's a bit tuckered out."

"You sure it's no bother to watch him?"

"No, ma'am. No bother at all. He listens real good. We're pals already."

"Make sure Vicki's dog doesn't disturb the other guests," Julie said, reaching down to pat Harvey's head.

"Yes, ma'am. He just stays by my side. You won't have to worry about him."

I gave Harvey a smooch on the nose and told him to be a good boy. He seemed to understand my words, and wasn't at all upset when we left. I was relieved that he didn't try to follow us.

Leon said in a firm tone, "Stay, boy." When I glanced back, Harvey was snoozing again.

When we got back to the B&B, Myra decided that she was tired and wasn't going to watch TV in the sitting room. I agreed that an early night was in order. I read for a while before turning out the light, then fell into a deep sleep.

Chapter 36

Saturday was filled with a variety of activities. Myra and I met for breakfast at 8:30, then we worked in the kitchen with Kate, Amanda, and Joe. Myra made several pies, and I prepped veggies for the evening meal.

Sister Cathy had given her approval for me to show Myra the basement bowling alley and tunnel after lunch. Kate wanted to join us, but a particularly crowded dining room negated that idea. Amanda promised to give Kate a tour when they weren't so busy.

Myra was like a kid in a candy store when she gawked at the wall of cabinets and vintage bowling alley. When I pointed out the nodule on the floor, she bent down to examine it. "You're right. This thing's barely visible."

I retrieved the decoy bowling pin from the cabinet and showed it to Myra, pointing out the groove on its bottom. When I removed the clothing bar and placed the pin on the bar holder, she shook her head in disbelief. I told her to press the button as I maneuvered the pin to open the hidden passage.

"I can't believe you figured this out," she exclaimed.

"I love solving a good puzzle."

She peered into the tunnel after I pulled the light switch. "This is amazing. How far does it go?"

"All the way beyond the parking lot."

"I can't walk that far."

"I know. I'll have Joe show you the pictures he took of JW's still."

We closed up the tunnel and I showed Myra the vintage bowling balls before we left. Like the rest of us had been, she was surprised that they were so heavy and had only two finger holes.

"It's too bad that all of this history is located under the main living quarters of the nuns," Myra said as we returned to the elevator. "A lot of people are going to want to see this stuff."

"I think the Sisters are hoping they can make just the outside barn with the still available for tours," I said. "But, quite honestly, I don't think they've figured out yet what they're going to do."

"You opened a can of worms."

"I guess I did."

^^^

Amanda and Kate were clearing tables in the dining room when Myra and I returned from our basement jaunt. Neither would accept our offer of assistance, assuring us that everything was under control. In fact, Cheryl had told them that they could have time at the lake after all of the guests had finished eating.

"What are your plans?" Amanda asked.

"I was hoping for some beach time as well," I said. "What about you, Myra?"

"I'm not sure I want to sit in the hot sun."

The three of us reacted as if with one voice, telling Myra that she *had* to experience one of most delightful amenities of the monastery. "You can sit in the shade near the tree-line," Kate said, "but you *have* to go."

Myra giggled like a schoolgirl, her eyes twinkling. "Well, then, I guess we're going to the lake."

"You're going to love it," Kate said with a huge grin. "And I'm sure Sister Julie will be happy to give you a ride in the golf cart. We'll help Joe finish up in the kitchen and meet you there."

Myra and I went upstairs to freshen up and change into beach attire, then headed to the gift shop. She wanted some kind of large brimmed hat, while I needed to see about our ride. Julie was busy with a customer, so we browsed while we waited.

After selecting one of the hats from the display, Myra set about finding souvenirs of her trip. She picked out a few jars of Julie's jellies, a couple of bottles of wine, and some postcards. By the time Julie was available, she had her purchases lined up on the counter.

"I can box these for you," Julie said. "I'm sure Joe wouldn't mind helping to load your car when you check out."

"Wonderful, though I'll take the hat with me now. We're heading to the lake for the afternoon."

"I'll drive you there as soon as Dolores returns. She's due back from her break shortly."

Myra chatted with Julie until another guest arrived. Once his poustinia reservation was processed, she offered him a ride to the cabin. He said he preferred to walk, obviously a returning visitor. Before long, Dolores arrived and we were on our way.

As Myra hopped into the golf cart, I told Julie that I'd been impressed by the smooth operations. She smiled proudly, happy that everything was coming together nicely.

"It's amazing, isn't it? Sometimes we mess up, but for the most part, we've got a good routine. Marian's always reminding us to work as a team."

"It's working," Myra agreed. "Every time Vicki would tell me her grand ideas to help the Sisters, I'd wonder how it could pan out. But you've done it."

Julie nodded with a chuckle. "Thanks, Myra. How about I pick you up at 4 p.m.?"

Myra and I spread our towels in a shaded section of the beach and lathered on the sunscreen. We watched as the sun's rays glistened across the water, casting bursts of colors like a gyrating prism. A flock of birds swooped to land on the other side of the lake, then flew off as a swarm only moments later. I wondered which one of them gave the signal that there were better pickings elsewhere.

"You're right," Myra said with a delightful expression. "It really *is* a magical place."

I nodded my agreement. We continued our nature watch until the young crowd arrived. Amanda and Joe sprinted past us, with Kate walking behind, chatting with Cheryl and Cathy. They stopped briefly to see if we wanted to join in their canoe race.

When we declined, Kate chirped, "Then it's settled. Nuns against chefs. The two of you can be judges."

Myra and I chuckled as we watched them drag the canoes to the water's edge and team up. Quite honestly, the nuns didn't stand a chance.

"You know what's nice?" Myra asked rhetorically. "I had never been around Sisters. I mean, I saw them portrayed on TV or the movies, like *Bells of St. Mary's*. That was a good one."

"What's your point?"

"They're not just holy rollers. They're real people with a special gift to bring out the best in others."

"I know what you mean, Myra. It's why this place is so special to me."

Myra nodded. She hit the nail on the head, summing my own experience better than I could. It wasn't the vineyards, or the lake, or the cabin that drew me back to the monastery, time and again. It was the Sisters. For a brief moment, I understood why Charlie felt he needed to follow Sister Tony to St. Louis.

The shadows lengthened as we watched the canoers rest their paddles, floating aimlessly in the center of the lake. Before we knew it, we heard the sound of chimes along with the sputter of the golf cart. Julie must have trolled the internet to find such a perfect new horn.

Laughing, we gathered our things and waved to the gang in the canoes. On the way back, I asked Sister Julie if she'd seen Leon and my dog in her travels. She pointed to the far field. Sure enough, there was Harvey, dutifully traipsing behind Leon as he pulled the weeds. My boy was in his glory.

Myra and I decided we had time for a short nap when we arrived at the B&B. The warm afternoon breezes had made us both drowsy. After thanking Julie for the ride, she told us that Sister Marian was hoping we'd join her table for supper. She and Sister Cathy would meet us at 6 p.m.

"We'd enjoy that," Myra said, without hesitation. "May I bring a bottle of wine to share?"

"One of the bottles you purchased earlier?"

"Add another to my tab. I want to celebrate this special weekend."

Chapter 37

Myra and I departed for home after brunch on Sunday. I walked over to Leon's cabin to get Harvey, brought him to the car, and pulled around to the monastery's *porte couchère* to pick up Myra. Kate had been keeping her company while she waited for me. After putting her grandmother's suitcase in the car, Kate gave Myra a hug and opened the car door.

"I had a wonderful time," Myra said. "Come see me soon."

"I promise. And I'll be sure to tell mom and dad that you behaved yourself this weekend."

"Very funny," Myra chuckled.

We waved goodbye and got on the road.

"I'm glad I had a chance to see Kate in action," Myra said. "You know, like in a professional way. Kids grow up so fast."

"It seems like only yesterday that she was just a toddler playing on your front lawn," I said, thinking back on those years. "Kate has become a fine young woman with a good head on her shoulders."

"I hope she meets a nice guy at college. I felt kind of sad for her on the lake yesterday. She was having a good time with Amanda and Joe, but you can tell she's a third wheel."

"I said the same thing to Charlie, just the other evening. Maybe I should talk to Amanda about it. You don't abandon your friends, even if you're falling in love."

"No, don't say anything to her. I wouldn't want it to strain their friendship. Kate didn't seem to have a problem with it. And, eventually, Amanda will realize the importance of maintaining relationships. Besides, I think that Kate's becoming friends with Sister Cheryl."

"I do, too. It's possible that Cheryl has also noticed that the budding chemistry between Amanda and Joe is distancing Kate. You're right, though. It won't be long before Kate goes off to school. She'll develop a whole new set of friends."

"I enjoyed the chance to get to know Sister Marian and Sister Cathy last evening. That Marian has a lot of ideas for the place, but she's wise. She's biding her time. Do you really think she'll sell off some of the land?"

"I was surprised when she mentioned that. She'll have to contend with Sister Tony."

"I think it's smart," Myra said. "They don't need all those acres, but they do need money—especially to do some of the projects she's planning. Anyway, I think she was fishing."

"What do you mean?"

"She was trying to get your reaction."

"I don't have a say in anything."

"You have a lot of experience in administration. Actually, they need someone like you on board. Yeah, maybe that's why she was throwing you bait. You know, like to see if you'd be interested."

"Interested in what?"

"I don't know. Maybe like being an executive director or some such thing."

"Were we at the same table last night? I didn't detect any fishing or any bait."

"Sister Marian didn't come out and say it," Myra said, "but you mark my words. They're going to ask you to be in charge of something."

"You're crazy."

"It makes sense. You have a lot of interest in the place. It was your idea to start the B&B and restaurant, and now the nuns have the dilemma of how to handle the historical items you discovered. I wasn't kidding when I said you opened a can of worms."

"They don't have to do anything about the still. Just keep it hidden in the woods."

"The cat's out of the bag," Myra said. "Who opened her big mouth to the folks at the historical society?"

"I didn't tell them about the still."

"I'm pretty sure you informed me that you mentioned the reason for your research when you went there, pal. They were darn quick to call Sister Marian and ask for a photo shoot of the bowling alley. Of course, by then you'd discovered the tunnel, which was pretty remarkable on its own merit."

Myra's words gave me pause. She was right that my ideas have had a snowball effect, impacting the lives of the Sisters in a big way. I glanced at Myra to see if she was teasing me, but she was watching the blur of the countryside as we drove by.

I knew that Myra had a talent for detecting innuendoes within a conversation. She saw or heard details that were often missed by those less perceptive. It's why she was so adept using psychology. In fact, I wondered if she had been playing a trump card with me. In other words, was she trying to get me to see something I was missing?

Once we got off the highway, slowing to the local speed limit, I added my two cents. "It seems to me, that you and Betty are in cahoots. She told me that I should retire out there in the country."

"I don't think you should retire there. You should get a job there."

"Now I know you're crazy. I have no desire to live in the boondocks."

"So you say, but you sure go there as often as you can get away. Besides, Harvey liked it there. I saw it myself."

We both laughed when Harvey responded with a hearty hound dog howl. Luckily, I pulled into Myra's driveway before the ridiculous conversation could go any further. At least, so I thought.

"You know what else I think?" Myra asked as she opened the car door.

"What?"

"You should ask the Sisters if you can buy a plot of their land and build your own home there. Right by the barn with the still. If you're lucky, you can have a lovely view of the pasture where Marian's going to put her goats."

"Enough!" I said. "Get out of here."

"I had a good time."

"I did, too. So glad you could come. I'll talk to you through the week."

The two of us were giggling as Myra rolled her suitcase to her front door.

Chapter 38

The month of August flew by like a swarm of bees chasing a running target. Charlie began calling me every couple of evenings, and I reciprocated almost as often. It seemed natural, and I enjoyed our conversations.

Mostly we talked about the monastery. Charlie enjoyed hearing stories about Amanda and the Sisters, and always asked about the B&B and restaurant. He wanted to know more about the still and the barn that housed it.

I reminded Charlie that I hadn't seen the building from the outside. In fact, I noted, it probably shouldn't even be called a barn, because it didn't seem that it had housed animals. At the same time, it was larger than a shed, and there was an old hay wagon on the upper level.

"Guess it could have been a machine barn," Charlie said. "It wouldn't have been unusual for a land owner to have a place to store large farming equipment. How close is it to the main road?"

"I don't really know. I'd say it's about the same distance as the mansion."

"The creek cuts in around there," Charlie said. "Might have been their water source."

"What do you mean?"

"The creek was dammed above the property to create the lake, but it actually meanders in and around the estate. You probably noticed it by the vineyard, along the drive to get to the lake."

"Sure. There's a fallen tree on the bank. I often sit there to rest if I'm out walking."

"The creek zigzags all over the place. There are actually several culverts along the main road."

"I never noticed," I said. "Did they need the creek water for making moonshine?"

"Probably. You might want to research that."

"I forgot to ask Sister Julie if I could look at some of the old recipes she found. I'll bet there's a bunch of them that they used to make their whiskey, or whatever they made."

"Yeah. You could check that out next time you're there."

"Betty and I booked our reservations for the last week of August."

"Good. In the meantime, see what you can find on the internet. How's the new guy working out?"

"Leon seems to be settling in. He watched Harvey for me when Myra and I spent the weekend at the B&B. I have to admit, Harvey liked him."

"You going to bring the dog when you go at the end of the month?"

"No. Myra's going to watch him. I don't want Harvey to wear out his welcome. Besides, Leon's going to be busy if he has to oversee the grape harvest."

I knew I shouldn't have mentioned anything connecting Leon with the responsibilities that Charlie previously held. Even if Charlie introduced the topic, he'd get quiet after my response. It would often be the signal that our conversation was over. The man could drive me crazy.

On evenings that we didn't chat, I did internet searches about prohibition, stills, and moonshine recipes. I learned that drinking alcohol was not a crime after the 18th amendment was enacted in early 1920. Only the manufacture, distribution, and sales of spirits were prohibited.

Oversight of illegal activity became the responsibility of individual states. Some strictly enforced the law, others were less vigilant. Regardless, federal agents were the watchdogs, and severe fines were levied if anyone was caught producing booze. While some Feds could be bribed, others would seek out potential sources of spirits, and destroy any equipment used in operations.

I found many pictures showing the Feds smashing jugs and axing barrels filled with moonshine. It was no surprise that JW went to a great deal of expense to hide his still. I wondered what kind of liquor he made.

Several historical websites attributed the passing of the 18th amendment to the need for grain to send to troops during World War I. Certainly the temperance leagues were vocal in their desire to rid communities of the scourge associated with drunkenness. The Women's Christian Temperance Union was a strong lobby to pass laws against alcohol use, but it was the powerful Anti-Saloon League that successfully made the United States a dry country. They obviously had no idea that it would be such a challenge to actually enforce the law.

I wondered if JW had grown his own grain, or if he purchased it from local farms. It made sense that the pasture Sister Marian wanted to use for goats could have been the site for growing rye or corn needed for the production of liquor.

I learned that a water source was an essential element in the moonshine business. Water was necessary for the distilling process. Barrels could be cooled in a stream after fermentation, and the used mash was often dumped into a creek.

Local folks might have thought that JW and Hildegarde purchased their property for its scenic value. I felt certain that the Smithfield's were enticed by the creek. They knew that the meandering stream was essential to their potentially profitable enterprise.

Chapter 39

Betty called a few days before we were planning to meet up at the monastery. Actually, we talked quite often. I'd been telling her about all of the things I'd learned about prohibition. As usual, she kept me grounded.

"Are you eating dinner?" she asked when I answered the phone. For some reason, Betty always checked to see if she was interrupting something important.

"No, still doing research."

"You must have filled a notebook, by now."

"How'd you guess? I'm going to wrap it as a gift for Sister Cathy."

"Have at it," Betty said. "She'll think it's her birthday. Are you packed yet?"

"Not yet. How about you?"

Betty replied that she'd thrown a few items into the open suitcase on the guest room bed. However, she wanted me to know that she was going to make next week a time for solitude.

Betty's comment surprised me since we had planned our vacation to coincide with the grape harvest. I wondered what had precipitated her announcement.

Betty explained that she was telling me ahead of time so she wouldn't hurt my feelings whenever she wanted to be alone. Nonetheless, she still wanted to help bring in the crop.

"It's no big deal, "Betty added. "I'm just not going to eat so many meals at the restaurant. No shopping trips, and no visits to the historical society. I want to get back to nature."

"I understand. I guess I've kind of embroiled you in all of the drama."

"It's not drama. I just don't have the same interest in the nun-stuff like you do. Give me the good old campsite."

"You missing John lately?" I asked.

"Yeah, I suppose I am. Yesterday was the anniversary of John's death. It's been five years. Hard to believe."

"Why didn't you tell me? We could have done something together."

"I needed to be alone. You know what I mean? Well, at least as alone as I could have been with three court appearances and a bunch of briefs to read."

"Oh, my! You *do* need a vacation."

"Definitely," Betty replied. "I'm glad you understand. But we'll still do the lake each day. That's really where I feel John's presence."

I told Betty how much I enjoyed her stories about John. I felt like I'd gotten to know him vicariously. It was often when we were sitting on the beach or canoeing on the water that Betty shared tidbits about their experiences. Some of those anecdotes had influenced me personally. More than Betty realized.

"On another note, have you chatted with Charlie lately?" Betty asked.

"Just about every evening this week. We've been trying to figure out what to do about the still."

"Do I have to remind you once again that it's not your business?" Betty asked. "Not yours and not Charlie's."

"I knew you were going to say that. But I feel like I'm the one who started this mess for the nuns. Besides, Charlie and I like trying to solve a problem together."

"Go at it, then. But I'm staying out of it."

I asked Betty if she remembered speaking to me about foundations. I told her that I was thinking more about it. Maybe even starting something that could support the preservation of local antiquities.

"Yeah. But you weren't interested."

"Well, I am now. In fact, that's what I was researching when you called. Anyway, it was Charlie's idea that we keep the historical aspects of the mansion apart from the monastery. In other words, the Sisters wouldn't have to be involved in giving tours or things like that."

"What would you call the foundation, and who's going to fund it?" Betty asked.

"I want to name it the Stella P. Munley Foundation for Local Historical Preservation. I'll start the base funding."

"Isn't that Charlie's wife? What's he think about that?"

"It is, but I haven't told him my whole plan yet. It's just beginning to gel in my head. Guess I'm going to need a lawyer."

"When he sues you for defamation or something?"

"No. To set up the non-profit corporation. Do you know anyone who can help me with it?"

"There are a couple of John's former colleagues who do that sort of thing. I can get you their contact information. But, I don't really understand where you're headed with this."

"I haven't figured it out yet. I'm thinking the foundation could pay out grants to do things like renovating the old barn, hire staff, and give tours of the still. Maybe even have some educational programming. I don't know."

"You don't want a foundation," Betty said.

"It was your idea in the first place."

"I know, but I've given it more reflection. A foundation provides charitable donations to other organizations. You *do* want a non-profit corporation, and you want to hire someone who can write grants to solicit funding for historic renovations and programs."

Betty's statement gave me pause. I realized that she was right and, after thinking about what she said for a few moments, I told her so.

"I also don't suggest that you name the corporation after Charlie's deceased wife, as thoughtful as that might be," Betty said. "Think about what you want the non-profit to be about. Could be something as simple as *The Smithfield Estate*, offering educational tours about the prohibition era. Maybe even about farming."

"I hadn't thought about farming," I said. "Amanda wants to have a farm-to-table theme for the restaurant. If we got volunteers, we could grow fresh fruits and vegetables. Sister Marian would love that."

"Who's *we*?" Betty asked.

"I mean the non-profit. I need to talk to Charlie about all of this."

"I think you need to talk to the Sisters about it," Betty said firmly.

"I will. As soon as Charlie and I work out the details."

"Here we go again," Betty intoned. "You can tell me all about it when we get to the lake on Saturday."

Chapter 40

After completing the check-in process, Sister Julie drove me to my poustinia in the golf cart so I didn't have to lug groceries. I wasn't planning to eat all of my meals in the cabin, but I did figure on breakfast and lunch. Maybe a couple of dinners. I wanted some quiet time to work on a grant.

After putting away the food, I changed into my bathing suit and walked to the lake. Betty was already sitting on her towel, gazing at a couple paddling a canoe.

"What took you so long?" she asked, as I settled myself on my towel and slathered on sunscreen.

"I stopped to see the kitchen crew to give them a care package."

"That was nice," Betty said. "...And?"

"You know me too well," I said with a chuckle. "And I gave Sister Marian the notes from my research and my proposal for the non-profit."

"Charlie thought it was a good idea?"

"Yeah. We worked on it every evening since I spoke with you. Even figured out who could be on the executive board. It's up to the nuns to decide if they want it to move forward."

"Did you pitch it to Sister Marian?"

"Not really. I just handed her the envelope and asked her to read it. It's just my way of trying to rectify the problems I've caused."

"You didn't cause the problems. You just stirred up the pot."

"Kind of like initiating the 18th Amendment," I said.

"In what way?"

"The idea behind prohibition might have been good, but it was a mess to enforce it, and it had disastrous consequences. Same thing with the B&B and restaurant, and now JW's still. I should have stayed out of it."

"That's what I told you."

"So, I'm trying to fix it."

Betty commented that she wouldn't put the B&B and restaurant in the same category as JW's bootleg operation. The B&B fulfilled a need for those who might want quiet time in a spiritual atmosphere. The restaurant made sense because the guests had to eat. Can't have them fixing their own meals in the kitchen. I agreed, but noted that it's all still overwhelming for the Sisters.

We watched the couple gliding smoothly across the lake as I expressed my interest in writing a grant proposal this week. I had found some funding support for historical renovations when searching the internet last week. Although I had never written a grant, it couldn't be that challenging. At least that's what I was thinking. Betty cautioned that the nuns may not be interested in getting financing for renovations.

"What's not to want? Charlie and I have it all spelled out for them."

"I remember a time when John had a similar idea," Betty said. "We were doing *pro bono* work for an inner city church. John figured that they could help more members of their congregation if they offered educational programs. He wanted to write a grant to fix up the basement of the church, make it into a lecture hall."

"That was a good idea," I said. "So, what happened?"

"John spent a lot of time working out the budget, getting speakers lined up, things like that. Unfortunately, the pastor didn't want it. Said his folks didn't want to sit and listen to some stranger preaching at them."

"So, his proposal just needed tweaking."

"No, they tossed it," Betty said.

"You preparing me for how I'm going to feel if the nuns toss my ideas?"

"Yep."

"Well, I'll find out tomorrow. I have a meeting with Sister Marian."

"Good luck," Betty said. It looked like she really meant it. "You want to take a spin around the lake?"

She and I dragged the canoe into the water and steadied ourselves. We were getting pretty adept at balancing the boat. I should speak for myself. Betty's always been good at it.

"You doing all right?" I asked as we paddled toward the raft in the middle of the lake. I knew this wasn't an easy time for her.

"I'm fine. Especially now that I can reconnect with John. I have a few things I want to talk to him about."

"Like what?"

"Like, should I move on?"

"Move on what?"

"Move on, like get serious with another guy," Betty said.

"You met someone?"

"I did. Actually, I've known him for a long while. Mike's a lawyer I work with. His wife died a couple of years ago. We've gone out a few times lately. I never really thought I could fall in love again. But now, I'm not so sure. I need to figure things out this week."

"You think John's going to send you a sign or something?"

"Guess you could say it that way. I just want to know if I should let Mike into my heart."

"I think John's going to tell you it's OK."

"We'll see," Betty said, as she glanced around the lake. "Is that Amanda's dad in the other canoe?"

Gazing in Betty's direction, I agreed that it looked like Steve Angeli. But there was a woman with him. I wasn't aware that he was dating seriously, or even that Steve would be here this week. Amanda hadn't mentioned it. Surely she'd have told me, unless she was upset that he had a lady friend.

Betty and I paddled closer, then rested our paddles so our canoe could drift towards theirs. Steve did the same.

"Good to see you both again," Steve said. "I'd like you to meet Hannah. She's staying in the B&B, and I'm in a cabin. Have to be a good example for my daughter."

We all laughed, then Betty and I introduced ourselves to Hannah. She seemed friendly and outgoing.

"You helping with the grape harvest this week?" I asked.

"Couldn't resist, especially after hearing you talk about it last year," Steve said.

"It won't be the same without your dad," I said.

"I'm sure. Did you know I flew out to St. Louis to see him a few weeks ago?"

"No. Neither Amanda nor Charlie mentioned it to me."

"It wasn't that big a deal," Steve said. "But we had a good time. Went up the Arch and saw some of the sights. I'd never been there before."

"I'm so glad. I do miss your dad."

"He misses you, too. Can't believe he told me that, but he did."

I was about to respond when I noticed Amanda, Joe, and Kate traipsing toward the lake. They seemed happy to have some time off before dinner service. We decided that they may want to use the canoes, so we headed back to shore.

"You going to be at supper tonight?" Steve asked us as he jumped out to help beach the canoes. Betty begged off, but I said I could plan on it.

"Great. Hannah and I would like you to join us. We have reservations for 6 p.m. We'll catch up with you then."

Betty and I greeted Amanda and her friends. When Steve and Hannah weren't looking, Amanda nodded to me and rolled her eyes. I laughed and told them all that I'd see them later.

As I gathered my stuff, Amanda was orchestrating a game of Frisbee with the whole gang. Her friendly inclusion of Hannah gave me a sense that they were going to be fine.

Chapter 41

Butterflies were creating havoc in my stomach when I arrived at the monastery for my meeting with Sister Marian. She had asked me to come to the Sisters' residence, and I rang their doorbell promptly at 3 p.m.

Sister Marian greeted me warmly, then brought me to the community room. I was surprised to see that Cathy, Cheryl, Dolores, and Julie were there, too. That made me really nervous. At least everyone looked relaxed in comfortable recliners, and they weren't staring at me down a long conference table.

Marian offered me a seat on the sofa. She said she wanted to have a group meeting to discuss my proposal. Evidently, she had made copies of it, because each of the Sisters had one in hand.

I felt kind of silly. Like I was again interfering in the nuns' lives. But, as I looked around, I didn't detect anything other than friendly faces.

I knew I should just be myself, while sharing what had precipitated my suggestions. I reiterated what I'd told Betty on the phone last week. That I wanted to try to fix the mess I had made. I figured that none of nuns wanted to be in the business of giving tours.

"Who spilled the beans?" Julie asked.

I didn't know what she was talking about. I suppose my expression betrayed my confusion.

"What Sister Julie means," Marian said with a comforting smile, "is that we've been having some discussions along these very lines. You've put a lot of work into your proposal and, quite frankly, you've gone beyond the things we've talked about."

"I didn't do it alone. Charlie and I have been putting our heads together to figure out a workable solution. I also shared my ideas with Betty, and she suggested some elements I hadn't considered."

I was aware that my comment about Charlie didn't go unnoticed. I distinctly saw Dolores nudge Julie, and she nodded in return.

"Let's review each of your suggestions and determine its feasibility," Marian said. "How about we begin with the non-profit organization? That could prove to be a little sticky since we're already a non-profit."

I explained that Charlie thought it was better to separate the congregation's non-profit status from the historical aspects of the estate. That's what had triggered my research.

"I'd considered starting a foundation that could fund the renovation of the barn housing JW's still. But, Betty made me realize that a foundation provides grants to other organizations. Plus, we wouldn't have the amount of funding needed to really get something like that off the ground. Some say that a healthy foundation begins with at least a million dollars."

"We thought of a foundation, also," Cathy said. "But we scratched the idea for the same reasons you did. I like the idea of a separate non-profit."

"As you saw in my proposal," I added, "I'm willing to hire a lawyer to draw up any legal documents and to file all of the required paperwork. Charlie and I came up with the names of people who might be willing to serve on the board although, of course, that would remain your decision. We think the chair of the board should be someone in your congregation who holds a position of authority.

Marian wanted to know more about the role of the non-profit organization. I told her that in addition to seeking grants to renovate historical aspects of the estate, we'd want to pursue educational ventures. A program about the 18th Amendment or the events that occurred as a result of prohibition might be interesting. Many of us only learned sketchy facts when we were in school.

"For example," I explained, "I thought it was totally illegal to drink any liquor during that period in our history. I learned, however, that it was actually the production and distribution of alcohol that was prohibited. Believe it or not, physicians could prescribe alcohol, and drug stores could dispense it."

"Interesting," Cheryl replied. "Would these programs be for children?"

"Educational programming would be age-related," I said. "If the barn with JW's still was a stop on a cultural tour with adults, certainly the content of the presentation would reflect that. But I can also envision a program that could be directed to children."

"Would the tunnel or bowling alley be a part of the tour?" Cathy asked.

"That would be your decision, of course. But, I think it could be, even though it's under your main living quarters. I'd suggest blocking off your trunk room. You have private stairs in that section of the convent that you could use, and it would be easy to add a wall in the basement."

"I don't know that I'd want a bunch of people traipsing through the convent," Dolores said.

"First of all, tours would have to be controlled," I noted. "You could limit the number of persons on a tour, as well as the number of tours each day."

Each of the Sisters nodded in agreement. Marian asked me to elaborate on my vision.

"I was thinking that the tour could start in the barn, once it's renovated. Guests could be led through the tunnel to see the vintage bowling alley, then brought up the elevator to pass by the gift shop on their way out."

"I like that idea," Dolores said. "Julie will have to make lots of jelly." We all laughed.

"And, if you want, visitors could be permitted to dine in the restaurant. Regardless, it would be good advertisement for the B&B."

"All of that has some appeal," Marian said, "but what's the part about farm-to-table?"

"That's for you," I said with a giggle. "I know you wanted goats, and you already have chickens. You could add a few cows, plant some crops. You know, stuff like that."

"We can't manage a farm," Marian replied emphatically.

"You wouldn't be doing it," I explained. "The non-profit would oversee it. Soliciting grants and donations could provide the funding. We'd get volunteers, maybe hire a staff person to do the actual farming. Start small and build up."

As I gazed around the room, the Sisters' expressions had turned to skepticism. I knew this idea was a stretch, but Charlie thought it was workable.

"You've got plenty of land, even if you decide to sell some of it. Now that I think about it, the non-profit could even rent the land from the Sisters."

"It doesn't make sense to me," Dolores said. "What's the purpose of having a working farm?"

"I have several reasons for the suggestion," I said. "The first one is educational. We're not so far from the city. Inner city schools look for places to have field trips. Learning experiences the kids might not ever have had. Cheryl's a teacher. She could be paid as a consultant for developing programs."

Cheryl nodded her agreement. "I like that. I can think of a lot of things to teach the kids."

"Our guests are here for peace and solitude," Julie said. "They want a place for reflection. We don't want a lot of children running around."

"You wouldn't see or hear visitors to the farm," I said. "You'd be developing the southwest part of the estate. There's plenty of land, and the trees would serve as a buffer. Charlie suggested a separate entrance from the main road."

"I guess that could work," Julie said. "What are your other reasons?"

"Father Jim's becoming a regular here. He could probably gather plenty of volunteers to help with planting and building fences. Betty and her husband used to take inner-city teens for camping trips in the country. The experience helped to develop them into successful young adults. And look at Leon and Charlie. They both have thrived here."

"It all really fits with our congregation's mission," Cheryl said.

"Definitely," I said with gusto. "And, Amanda had wanted a farm-to-table theme for the restaurant. Couldn't be anything closer than a farm on the property."

I could have gone on, but I didn't want to overwhelm the Sisters. They were definitely mulling my words.

"What would we call this non-profit?" Marian asked.

"That, too, would be your decision," I replied. "It could be something like *Smithfield Estate* or *Smithfield Creek*. Whatever it is, you want a name that reflects both the historical aspect of the property, as well as the educational opportunities of a farm."

"The county commissioners might frown on us changing the name of the creek," Julie said. "It's called Rock Creek."

Dolores rolled her eyes. "So we use the correct title in whatever name we choose. It's no big deal."

"You've certainly given us a lot to think about," Marian said. "I know Cathy wants more time to review the financial spreadsheet that you've included. But I have one more question for you. If we agreed to your proposal, would you consider a full-time position as managing director?"

Despite Myra's prophesy, I was absolutely floored. Quite honestly, I'd thought that Charlie could oversee the operations, although I hadn't mentioned that to him yet. I didn't even know if the possibility would entice him to return.

"I don't know," I said after a long pause. "I was thinking I could write grants for you during my evenings or on weekends at home, while retaining my current position at the publishing firm. Besides, I'm getting close to retirement age. You don't want some old geezer running the place."

"Age isn't an aspect that we consider," Julie said with a chuckle. "Some of our Sisters are in their late 70's, and they're still quite active. Some even hold positions in administration."

"We wouldn't ask you to accept the job if we didn't think you were the right person for it," Marian said. "In fact, we've had a lot of strategic planning meetings to try to figure out a way to separate all of the historical aspects of the estate from our mission as religious. Your name came up in every one of those discussions, and that's before we even received your proposal. In fact, I've already asked permission of our administration in St. Louis to sell some acreage and offer you a substantial salary."

"Yeah, we figured you probably have a pretty good income, being a VP and all," Julie said. "We're willing to match it. And you could even bring your dog." Everyone laughed.

"I don't know what to say."

"Can't believe you're speechless," Sister Marian said with a chuckle. "You're usually pretty good with words."

My thoughts were a jumble. I was completely thrown off-guard with the realization that the Sisters had already planned many of the things Charlie and I had discussed. I wanted to make it clear, though, that the non-profit would be soliciting grants to pay for a director. The nuns wouldn't need stretch their budget.

"We realize that," Sister Cathy replied. "And we'd have to look into the legality of our paying you, at least initially, so we don't blend the non-profits. In any case, we think we need to hire you sooner, rather than later.

Cheryl added her two cents. "In addition, you'll need a place to live. We wouldn't want you to commute from town, and we think the B&B or a poustinia wouldn't be appropriate. When we sell some of our land, we'll build a modest home for you, not too far from JW's barn."

"I'm quite honored," I replied. "But I really need to mull about this."

"Understandable," Marian said with a broad smile. "We'll do the same. You've included elements in your proposal that we haven't fully considered. Since you'll be here through the week, we can reflect on our options and make a collaborative final decision before you leave."

"Agreed," I said, shaking my head at the enormity of the decision. "In the meantime, is Leon ready for the grape harvest? I'll be happy to help him."

"We're all set," Marian said. "We're just grateful to have extra hands in the vineyard. The more, the merrier, I say."

"Do you want to join us for Vespers?" Cheryl asked.

"I don't think so. I have a lot of pondering to do."

As I was walking back to my poustinia, I was grateful that my proposal hadn't been axed. In fact, I'd be happy to tell Betty that my ideas were being seriously considered. Charlie would be pleased about it, too.

But I didn't want to say anything about the Sisters' offer to either of them yet. How in heaven's name would I have the courage to submit my resignation at the firm and move to the boondocks?

Chapter 42

I tossed and turned all night. It was still dark when I put the kettle on and brought a cup of tea to my porch. I watched the sky lighten with a few golden streaks, and heard the distant crowing of the rooster. I wondered if he was sharing his enthusiasm at beginning a new day, of if he was reminding me that I didn't enjoy rising with the birds.

I began to make a list of pros and cons of the Sisters' offer in my mind. I lost track of how many of each I had considered, but it seemed to me that the cons were winning. Lack of sleep was playing havoc with my disposition, and I didn't like the feelings I was experiencing.

Whenever I awoke with unsettled emotions, I could trace it back to a bad decision I had made at work, and then rectify it. This was different. I wasn't sure what to do.

I took a shower, hoping the warm water would calm my frazzled nerves. After dressing, I walked along the road until I came to the fallen tree by the creek. Betty always said that she would use this serene location to debrief from her usual hectic pace.

I listened to the sounds around me, and watched little bubbles arise every so often to the surface of the stream. I began to imagine Hildegarde sitting in this very spot, maybe troubled by a disagreement with JW, or a spat among the servants. I closed my eyes, wishing I had someone to help me discern what to do.

I heard the distinct crunch of a stick on the ground, and turned to see Steve approaching. He looked as surprised as I was to meet anyone in this quiet spot. "I didn't mean to startle you," he said. "I didn't think anyone would be here so early in the morning."

"Just clearing my brain."

"Me, too. I found this site last time I was here. Good place to cogitate."

"Everything OK?"

"I don't know. Didn't sleep at all last night. Joe asked my permission to propose to Amanda."

"I wondered when Joe would pop the question. It's clear that they've fallen in love."

"Guess I didn't see it coming. At least not yet. They're too young."

"Probably not much younger than you were when you married Amanda's mother."

"Yeah, but that was different. We both had common sense. Amanda's my baby girl."

"Amanda's grown up now. She's more mature than you might think, especially after all she's been through this year. And Joe's a very responsible young man. How'd you respond to him?"

"I gave my approval, but now I'm wondering if I did the right thing."

"Would you rather they just live together? Because that's probably going to happen sooner or later."

"No, of course not. I just think I'll be kicking myself for saying yes if it doesn't work out."

"None of us knows what the future will bring. We have to make decisions based on our present reality. I understand that you want the best for Amanda. I'm also pretty sure she's already decided that Joe is perfect for her."

"You think I was right to approve?"

"I do."

"Why am I so uneasy about it? I barely slept a wink."

"Because you still think of Amanda as your little girl, and you want to protect her. Your emotions are valid, Steve. This is a new transition in your life, and it's not easy."

"You can say that again. Guess I'm facing a couple of big changes."

Steve told me that he and Hannah were getting serious. He thought this would be a good time to bring Hannah to the monastery, and introduce her to Amanda. There'd be plenty of activities this week, and he was hoping Amanda and Hannah would get to know each other.

"How's that going?" I asked.

"Guess it's pretty good. We've all had a nice time at the lake the last few afternoons. Hannah said she watches TV with Amanda and Joe in the evenings after they close out the kitchen. Doesn't seem like any problem there."

"Did Amanda know about Hannah before this week?"

"No, I didn't know how to broach the subject. I mean, she knew I was dating, but I never mentioned anyone in particular. Do you think she's ready to accept Hannah as my wife?"

"Not yet. You know Amanda. She has to get used to an idea before she can embrace it. Otherwise, she'll dig in her heels and resist."

"I was worried about that," Steve said.

I told Steve that he was smart to bring Hannah to the B&B. Amanda's no dummy. She's probably aware that Hannah's special enough that her dad wanted them to meet. If Amanda likes Hannah, he'll know it. Steve seemed relieved that he was at least on the right track.

"When's Joe going to propose to Amanda?" I asked.

"Tomorrow afternoon, at the lake. He's going to take off work at the diner for a few days so he can help get ready for the harvest. Joe wants me to help him pick out a ring when he gets off work today. Geez!"

"That's great! A little male bonding with your future son-in-law."

"Hannah's coming, too. I figured she could add a woman's perspective. Besides, I'll see the types of settings that she likes. Killing two birds with one stone. Get it?"

I laughed and told Steve that I'd make sure to be on the beach for the momentous occasion. He seemed relieved to have additional support.

As I walked back to my cabin, I realized that I was feeling much better. Helping someone else always takes us out of our own small world. Makes us more aware that our own problems are miniscule compared to what others might be facing.

I thought about my words to Steve. That we don't know what the future will bring. We have to live in the moment. I knew for certain that what I said had meaning for me, as well. I'd be able to discern the answer to my own dilemma by the end of the week.

Chapter 43

Betty and I went canoeing the next afternoon. While we rested from paddling, I told her that Sister Cathy gave me one of the cartons that Julie had found in the mansion basement. I spent last evening going through all of the recipes.

Many appeared to be instructions for different liquors, though none of them were labeled. Also, they were written in a very fancy script which made them difficult to read. Regardless, I explained, it was rather easy to separate the recipes for jams or jellies from the others.

"How's that?" Betty asked.

"Alcoholic beverages use yeast and some form of grain, in addition to sugar and fruit. The grapes were readily available for business once Hildegarde's vines started producing, and I suspect they grew corn and rye on the estate."

"I remember my mother making root beer when I was a kid," Betty said. "She used an extract that she'd purchase, then add sugar, yeast, and water. She saved all kinds of soda bottles through the year, would wash them, and then fill them with the concoction. After capping the full bottles, she'd lay them on the grass in the sun, and in about 2 weeks they were ready to drink."

"Did it taste like root beer?" I asked.

"It was powerful stuff, kicked a punch. Guess it was somewhat alcoholic, too. My friends thought it reminded them of real beer. Funny thing though, if those bottles stayed in the sun too long, they'd explode. Kind of like a warm bottle of soda when you shake it up. We kids would all laugh; my mother, not so much."

"That's a riot," I said. "One of the recipes I found called for rye, corn, grapes, sugar, and yeast. Those were put in a barrel and warm water was added. Then the barrel was kept warm for 5 days for the concoction to ferment. Kind of like your mother's root beer."

"Then it was ready?"

"No. That was the mash. They had to strain the juice from the mash, and cook it in the still. As it evaporated, it would drip into copper piping that flowed through a barrel filled with cold water. It eventually came out of the spigot, into the jug placed on the floor. Apparently, that made 100 proof whiskey."

"Wow. Then they'd toss the mash?"

"They could use the same mash about three times, then they'd clean out the barrel in a stream."

"No wonder they needed a creek on the estate," Betty said.

"Exactly. They could also make bourbon by adding some concentrated citrus juice for flavor and color. I'd like to copy the recipes I found, and try to make some of them in JW's still."

"It could be a great educational program if there were tours like you had in your proposal. How'd your meeting go with Sister Marian the other day?"

"Pretty good. But the discussion also included Dolores, Cathy, Cheryl, and Julie."

"That must have been a bit overwhelming. Did they like your suggestions?"

"Some of them. They're considering the others."

"So, they didn't scrap it?"

"No," I chuckled. "In fact, they said they've been thinking along the same lines."

I explained that the Sisters liked the idea of setting up the non-profit separate from the congregation. In fact, that part of the proposal was approved. They needed more time to decide if they wanted to offer tours through the mansion, though they seemed to agree that those might help advertise the B&B and restaurant.

"How about the farm?" Betty asked.

"They're thinking about that, too. It's beyond anything they'd considered. I'm not sure they got the connection."

"All of this is probably overwhelming to them. It takes time to process."

"More than you can imagine," I said, thinking about my own dilemma. "How about we go back to the beach now?"

"What's your hurry? Drifting on the lake is very relaxing."

"Amanda and Joe will be taking their break soon. They'll probably want to use the canoe."

"They can use the other one."

"Steve and Hannah plan to use that one."

Betty didn't seem too happy about it, but she joined in the paddling back to shore. I didn't tell her that Joe was going to propose to Amanda, and that I wanted to witness it. After all, he could get cold feet, and I'd be the one who spilled the beans.

∧∧∧

Betty and I spread our towels under the shade of the trees. It wasn't long before Steve and Hannah arrived. We invited them to sit with us, but Steve told us that they wanted to get some sun.

"The canoe's available," Betty noted.

"Later," Steve said, as he and Hannah settled themselves on the sand.

"We could've stayed on the lake," Betty complained.

"We're fine here."

Amanda and Joe arrived shortly, galloping towards the lake. They waved as they passed us, then dragged the canoe to the water's edge, not too far from Steve and Hannah. Joe won the race by only a hair, though Amanda contested the results by saying that Joe cheated.

"You and Hannah canoeing, Dad?" Amanda asked.

"In a few minutes," he said.

Betty and I watched the scene unfold as Joe squatted on the sand, reaching into his shoe. Then, he got on one knee before Amanda.

"What are you doing, Joe? Hurry up."

Hannah and Steve both had their cell phones geared for taking photos. The special moment happened so quickly, I was kicking myself for not being ready.

Joe held up the ring and, in a voice pulsing with emotion, said to Amanda, "Will you marry me?"

"Oh, my gosh," Betty whispered, grabbing my hand.

Amanda screamed, "Yes! Oh, yes!"

Joe put the ring on Amanda's finger, and embraced her. After a long kiss, they turned to the rest of us. I could see tears glistening on Amanda's face. I had never seen her so happy.

"You knew?" she said to her father.

"Of course I did. I gave my approval. Right, Joe?"

"Without a moment's hesitation," Joe agreed.

Amanda ran to her dad, giving him a big hug and kiss on the cheek. She even hugged Hannah, then showed them the ring. As if suddenly remembering that Betty and I were also present, Amanda grabbed Joe's hand and they sprinted toward us.

I hugged them both, and said all the appropriate words while Amanda held out her hand for us to see the ring. Before I knew it, they were kissing again.

"You two have a lot to talk about," I said with a chuckle. "I think Betty and I are going to head back to our cabins."

"You going to the restaurant tonight?" Amanda asked. "I'd like you both to be there. I mean, like it's a special night and all."

I looked at Betty, and she nodded her approval.

"Yes, we'll be there to celebrate your special occasion."

"Awesome," Amanda said, as she pulled Joe back to the canoe. "We'll catch you later."

Betty and I waved to Steve and Hannah, and gathered our things. As we walked through the trees, I glanced at Betty and saw that she was crying.

"What's the matter with you?" I asked. "I hope those are tears of joy."

"For sure. That's the sign I've been waiting for."

Chapter 44

Steve and Hannah insisted that Betty and I sit at their table for supper. I thought it'd be nice to get to know Hannah a little better, especially since it probably wouldn't be too long before they, too, decided to tie the knot. Of course, I kept that tidbit to myself.

Hannah was a good talker, as opposed to Steve, who was typically as quiet as his father. Hannah seemed to be about the same age as Steve, early forties I'd guess, and had never married. When I asked her about it, she said she hadn't met the right guy. I could definitely identify with that.

They showed Betty and me the pictures on their phones that they had taken of Joe's proposal. Steve even captured a short video of Amanda's response. It was priceless.

"I forwarded the photos to Amanda and Joe," Steve said. "Apparently, they've already been uploaded to Facebook and Instagram." We all laughed.

"Good thing it's not too crowded here tonight," I said, glancing around the room. "I imagine that Amanda and Joe are having a difficult time staying focused on food service."

"A lot of the nuns ate earlier," Hannah said, "though I think Sister Cheryl is helping in the kitchen."

"Yeah," Steve said, following my gaze. "After they finish plating the final orders, everyone's going to join us for dessert. We can push a couple of tables together."

I thought that was a nice way to celebrate Amanda and Joe's engagement. We chatted about when they might plan to have their wedding, where it might be, and where they might live, none of which Amanda had probably yet had time to consider.

After Cheryl brought our dinners, I changed the topic to the next day's grape harvest. I knew it would be a challenge for Leon to orchestrate everything, but figured the Sisters would be helping him.

Betty recalled how difficult it had been to work in the hot sun last summer. I agreed, but said that I particularly liked the camaraderie among the workers. In fact, I enjoyed it so much that I stayed for the second harvest the following week.

"You probably just wanted to hang out with my dad," Steve said with a wide grin.

"Very funny. I barely knew him then. But I was impressed with how well he organized the harvest. And I really enjoyed the luncheon that the Sisters prepared for everyone afterwards. I wonder if they'll do that this year."

"They're planning on it," Steve said. "Hannah's going to help Amanda set up the dining room later."

"They were prepping for it last night," Hannah added. "Seems like they have everything under control."

"Marian told me the other day that Leon will be fine," I said. "But, I don't know. It's just going to be weird without Sister Tony and Charlie."

"It's not your worry," Betty reminded me.

"I know. I'm just saying."

When we finished eating, Cheryl arrived to bus our table. Joe and Steve worked together to rearrange the seating. Hannah went to the gift shop to tell Julie and Dolores that we were about ready for dessert.

It seemed a good time to go to the kitchen to get Amanda, but Joe insisted that I had to wait. The happy couple planned to make a grand entrance.

Before long, Sister Marian arrived with a large sheet cake that she placed in the center of the long table. It was beautifully decorated with icing flowers and scripted with congratulations. In no time, the other Sisters joined us, looking quite proud that they'd been able to pull together the impromptu gathering.

Cheryl brought small plates to the table, then announced the arrival of our special guests. Amanda and Joe pushed open the kitchen door, and everyone cheered.

Standing behind them was Charlie. I gasped, and my eyes filled with tears.

^^^

While Amanda and Joe took their seats, Charlie came over to me and said something corny like I looked more beautiful than ever. I arose from my chair, and threw myself into his arms. I'd have to admit, it was a pretty amazing kiss.

Realizing that everyone was gawking at us, Charlie and I composed ourselves and took a seat. I suppose we were both a little embarrassed, but the others were enjoying my reaction.

"You look surprised," Sister Cathy said with a giggle, her eyes twinkling.

"I can't believe it," I sputtered. Charlie squeezed my hand.

"It's not easy pulling one over on you," Amanda said. Her expression made me laugh.

"So, your engagement was just a ploy?" I asked.

"No way. Just happened to be good timing. I had the heck of a time figuring out how to get you to dinner tonight."

I turned to Charlie, not wanting to take my eyes off him. "When did you arrive?"

"This morning. Sister Marian picked me up at the airport. After we stopped at a bakery to buy the cake, we spent most of the day planning the harvest."

"How long are you staying?"

"Forever, I hope."

"Oh, my gosh," I cried. Literally.

Charlie reached over to give me another kiss, but I made sure that it was a modest one. We were in a room filled with nuns. Cheryl began distributing the cake.

"We've been planning this for a while, you know," Charlie said. "Once you and I worked on the proposal for the Sisters, I knew where my heart was."

"Right," Julie nodded. "So, when you were telling us how Charlie was involved with some of your suggestions, we already knew that he'd be here to organize the harvest."

"You're all devious," I said.

"In a good way," Dolores chirped.

"What about Leon?" I asked.

"He's going to help Charlie. He'll learn the ropes and be able to take charge next year."

"Yeah, but Charlie's going to stay."

"They'll both be busy with the farm," Marian said.

"Wow!" I exclaimed. "You've decided?"

Betty gave me a thumbs up. Sister Marian said that the Sisters' vote was unanimous. In fact, their administration team approved the proposal yesterday.

"Tours and everything?" I asked.

"That depends on you," Marian said.

Betty looked at me, not sure what was being discussed. Amanda also didn't know what was going on, and she was quite vocal about it.

I looked into Charlie's eyes, and saw his encouragement. I knew in a second that this was what I wanted to do, where I wanted to be.

"My answer is yes," I said simply.

The nuns cheered. Amanda, looking confused, said, "Yes to what?"

"What's the name going to be?" I asked Marian.

"*Rock Creek Farm.*"

"Yes to being the managing director of *Rock Creek Farm.*"

Chapter 45

I knew I had caused quite a stir with my announcement last evening. Betty and Amanda had given me that *why didn't you tell me* look, but I explained that it had been a really difficult decision. In fact, I was amazed that the words had come out of my mouth so easily. Despite the challenges ahead, I was certain that I belonged here, working side by side with the Sisters, and forging a new life with Charlie.

We had all lent a hand to set up the dining room for the harvest luncheon, then Charlie walked with Betty and me to our cabins. After making sure that Betty got to her poustinia safely, Charlie joined me on my porch.

I made us each a cup of tea, and we sat quietly listening to the cicadas and watching the fireflies. Putting my hand on his, I told Charlie how happy I was that he was home. He expressed how much he had missed me. He said he'd wanted to return to the monastery, but was afraid that I'd reject him.

I knew that leaving Sister Tony in St. Louis had to have been difficult for him. Charlie had identified Tony with Stella. I figured his decision to return also signified that he was ready to move forward. I was ready, too.

We made it an early night, knowing that Charlie would be up very early to prepare for the harvest. He was bunking on a cot in Steve's cabin, and meeting Leon at 6:00 a.m. Laborers didn't have to be there until 7:00.

The next morning, Betty and I walked to the vineyard together. She wanted to know if I got any sleep last night. I told her I'd slept like a baby, which was rather surprising given all that happened yesterday. She said she felt all along that Charlie would be back.

"I feel kind of bad that I didn't tell you about the Sisters' offer," I said. "I was overwhelmed and needed to mull."

"Thought you didn't want to live in the boondocks."

"It's different now that Charlie returned. Did you know he'd be here for the harvest?"

"Yeah. Sister Julie told me yesterday morning when I was taking a walk. She wanted me to make sure that you'd be at the restaurant for dinner, but made me swear I wouldn't tell you why. It worked out perfectly when Joe proposed to Amanda. I assume you knew about that."

"Only because Steve mentioned it to me the day before. He was hoping he made the right decision to give his approval."

"I've never seen Amanda so happy," Betty said. "I think she and Joe make a great couple. They're perfect for each other."

"What about you?" I asked. "You said something about a sign."

"I've had some talks with John this week. I don't mean like I'm crazy or anything. Just wanted him to let me what I should do about Mike. Did I ever tell you how John proposed to me?"

"Don't think so."

"We went camping at a lake. He asked me to marry him on the beach, at sunset. It was very romantic."

"So Joe's proposal to Amanda was similar to John's."

"Yeah."

"How's that a sign? You think John doesn't want you to move on?"

"He wants me to remember why I loved him so much. That what we had was special."

"It doesn't mean you can't be open to a different kind of special."

"I know that," Betty said, nodding her head. "I've decided that I'm going to continue dating Mike, but I'm not going to rush things. Our relationship will evolve over time. Besides, I think I'm going to be pretty busy going to weddings this year."

We both chuckled as we joined the crew arriving for the harvest.

^^^

Like last year, the grapes in the section of the vineyard that had more direct sun were ripe before the others. There would have to be another harvest next week.

Charlie showed Leon, and the others who hadn't been there before, how to snip the ripened grape clusters to avoid bruising the fruit. Initially, Charlie walked the field with Leon, demonstrating how to encourage the workers to maintain a steady pace. Eventually, Charlie persuaded Leon to take on that responsibility entirely.

Charlie stayed at the collecting station, distributing new baskets as filled ones were brought to him. When Charlie called for a break, he and Leon disbursed cold bottles of water to each harvester. Finally, Charlie declared that the day's work was finished. He invited all of us to the restaurant dining room for lunch.

This was my favorite part of the harvest. Charlie and I sat next to two migrant workers, and across from Leon and three others. Everyone mixed and mingled. It was a diverse group, and

I enjoyed chatting with each person. I was rather surprised to see Kate in the crowd but, like Joe, she said she had taken off work to help Amanda prepare the food for the buffet.

I figured that Sister Tony had mentored Marian, because she welcomed us and thanked us for our work before saying a prayer of blessing. She also presented each person with his or her wages for the day, though most of the home guard declined theirs.

Before the migrant laborers departed, Charlie reminded them that there'd be another harvest next week, same day, same time. I was tempted to tell him that I'd stay an extra week like I did last year, but I had a lot of things to do at home if I was going to get my house on the market.

As the visitors dispersed, I watched Amanda show Kate her engagement ring. Kate didn't look surprised to see it, so I felt sure that Amanda had called her last night. Kate *did* give her an enthusiastic hug, and I heard her say how thrilled she was for Amanda and Joe.

Some of the Sisters began clearing tables, but a few of us went back for iced tea. Leon and Charlie helped themselves to seconds at the buffet, and returned to the table. Betty, Steve, and Hannah joined us, too.

"How'd it go, Leon?" I asked.

"OK, I guess. I'm pretty pooped."

"You did real good," Charlie said. "Think you can handle it yourself next week?"

"Don't know, sir. Might not be here."

"Of course you will," I said. "Charlie needs you."

"No, ma'am. I think I'd best be leaving so he can get back into his cabin."

I started to respond, but Charlie interrupted. "Not so fast, Leon. I'll be getting married to Vicki, if she'll have me."

I choked on my tea, as everyone in the room got quiet. If that was Charlie's proposal, it didn't have the romantic quality that I had expected. Joe would have to teach him a thing or two.

"You proposing, dad?" Steve asked.

"Guess I am. What do you say, Vicki?"

"That's not how you do it, GP," Amanda said from across the room. "You need to get down on one knee. Like they do in the movies. And you need a ring to put on Vicki's finger."

I looked at Betty and rolled my eyes. She was trying hard not to laugh. Charlie asked Amanda if he could borrow her ring, just for a moment. Amanda took off her ring, and handed it to her grandfather.

To everyone's delight, Charlie bent down on one knee in front of me. Gathering his courage, he took my hand. "Will you marry me?"

I gazed into Charlie's eyes, taking extra time to respond. I guess it made him more nervous than he already was, but I wanted him to know that this was a big deal for me. Charlie held Amanda's ring in front of me, like he was offering it as bait.

Finally, I replied, "Yes, Charlie. I'll marry you."

Everyone cheered as Charlie tried to put Amanda's ring on my finger. It didn't fit. We were laughing so hard that we could barely kiss.

I handed the ring back to Amanda, then turned to Leon, "Looks like you'll have to stay. Charlie and I have a wedding to plan."

Chapter 46

After the hoopla died down, Charlie stayed to show Leon how to help prepare the grapes to be sent out for wine production. Betty and I weren't needed, so we strolled back to my place, laughing all the while.

"Just think about all the stories you can tell your future great-grandkids," Betty said. "The day GP proposed to me..."

"Not quite like the romantic sunset you had."

"Obviously not," she replied, smothering a giggle. "But you'll never forget it."

"I have a feeling that my life with Charlie will be like that. One surprise after another."

"You didn't know he was going to propose?"

"I don't think he knew it himself."

"It's a sign," Betty said. "You're meant to be together."

"More like an indication that I'm crazy, but you often tell me that. Seriously, I do love Charlie. I'm glad all of the drama of wondering if or when he'd propose is over. Now we can just get on with planning the wedding."

When we reached my poustinia, Betty and I rested on the porch rocking chairs. I pointed out the two chipmunks that often scurried around the bushes. They seemed to enjoy my company.

"Get used to them," Betty said with a chuckle. "You'll have plenty of wildlife friends around here. You going to see Charlie later?"

"He's coming over after he shows Leon how to process the grapes."

"I can't believe that Leon was thinking about taking off."

"Me either. It seemed like Leon's happy here, but maybe he doesn't feel that he's needed. I've got to reinforce how crucial he is. We'll especially need his help when we start clearing the woods and restoring JW's old barn."

Betty suggested that Leon might be lonely. That didn't seem likely, given the lifestyle that Leon seemed to prefer. Still, I remembered that Leon had enjoyed Harvey's companionship. Maybe I could entice him to take care of Harvey while I got my house ready to sell.

"Couldn't hurt to ask," Betty said. "You and Charlie going to rent a place in town?"

"He doesn't know it yet, but we're going to build a home on the estate. Over where the farm will be located."

"You're going to be living in the boondocks."

"I know. Ironic, isn't it?"

"Very. But I think it's perfect," Betty said.

^^^

Charlie arrived shortly after Betty departed, with two bottles of soda in hand. He opened one and handed it to me. "I guess I messed up today," Charlie said, uncapping his bottle and taking a swig.

"You rescinding your proposal?"

"No way. I just didn't make it very romantic. You sure you want to marry me?"

"I'm positive."

"I need to get you an engagement ring. I was going to do that before I proposed, but then it all just sort of happened."

"I'm glad that part's over," I said. "Now we can plan our future."

"I agree. When do you want to get married?"

"I don't know. Soon, I guess. What about you?"

"How about this weekend?" Charlie asked.

"Are you kidding?"

"Not really," Charlie said. "Think about it. Everyone we'd want to witness our wedding is already here. Well, not Tony, but that's OK. She gave me her blessing."

I gazed into the trees as I mulled. Charlie was right. I didn't want anything extravagant. I'd want to get married at the monastery, anyway. And, it would certainly simplify matters if we could just tie the knot and be done with it.

"You thinking?" Charlie asked.

"Yeah. It's not a bad idea. Actually, I agree with you. The only problem might be the wedding license. How long's it take to get one?"

"Didn't take any time at all when I married Stella. But that was 40 years ago. We could check it out at the town hall."

I looked at my watch. If we hurried, we could get there before it closed. "Let's go," I said.

The actual process for obtaining the license wasn't bad at all. Charlie and I presented our drivers' licenses, and the staff person verified through documents on-line that neither of us had impediments for marriage. Charlie paid the fee, while we were told that the license was good for 60 days.

As we got back into the car, I said, "We're going to have to ask Sister Marian if we can use the chapel on Saturday morning."

"You want a church wedding?"

"I'd like a monastery wedding. I wonder if Father Jim would witness our vows."

"Isn't he the priest in charge of the shelter?" Charlie asked.

"Yes. And, as Amanda would say, he's awesome. I'll ask Joe for his contact number and call him tonight."

"Guess I need to get you a wedding band, too. You want to come with me tomorrow to pick out your rings?"

"You don't have to get anything expensive."

"I've been saving for them. A long time. We can go to the outlet mall. I'm pretty sure they have a jewelry store there."

"You can help me select your wedding band, too. While we're at the mall, I'll get a new dress and you can get a nice suit."

"I think we're ready," Charlie said.

"Just about," I agreed. "We'll definitely have it together by Saturday."

Chapter 47

We made it back in time for supper at the restaurant. Charlie and I saw Sister Marian leaving the gift shop, so I asked her if the chapel was available on Saturday morning. I told her that we'd decided to have the wedding this weekend, before everyone departed.

Although surprised, Marian was wonderfully gracious. She suggested that we plan on 11:00 a.m., noting that Father Jim would be saying Mass for the Sisters at 9:30.

"That's great that Father Jim will be here this weekend," I said. "I was hoping he'd officiate."

"I'm sure he'd be honored to participate in your special day," Marian said. "I have his number on my cell phone in case you want to call him. Have you told the others yet?"

"We haven't told anyone else yet because we wanted to check with you first, but I definitely want Father Jim's number. Would we be able to have a small reception in the dining room afterwards?

"If you don't mind having guests of the B&B join you," Marian replied. "In fact, Jeff and Kim have reservations for this weekend."

"Fabulous," I said. "We'd really like them to be part of the celebration."

Charlie agreed. "Just so you know, we'll be paying for any catering.

"We can talk about all of that later," Marian said. "I'd also like to meet with the two of you to plan the initial steps of our project. Would you be available on Friday afternoon?"

We agreed on the time, and I told Marian that we'd have details worked out by then. In the meantime, we needed to let everyone know about the wedding.

When we joined Steve and Hannah for supper, Charlie immediately announced our plans to them. He tried to keep his voice controlled, but his enthusiasm was infectious.

"You two don't waste time," Steve chuckled. "You afraid she's going to get away, dad?"

"If I hadn't been so stubborn, we could have wrapped this up a while ago," Charlie said. "Besides, no use waiting. We're not getting any younger."

"What about a marriage license?" Steve asked.

"Got it."

"Wow. That's amazing. You going to borrow Amanda's ring again?"

"No, wise guy. Vicki and I are going shopping tomorrow."

"You better tell Amanda before she hears it from anyone else," Steve noted. "She'll be mighty upset if she's not one of the first to know."

"We'll tell her after supper," I said.

"I'm not kidding," Steve warned.

Though Charlie and I knew Steve was right, we both felt awkward about causing any inconvenience. Hannah suggested that Steve get Amanda to come to our table.

When Steve returned with Amanda, she glanced at our expressions, wondering what was so important to require her immediate attention. "What's up, guys?"

"GP and I have set a date for our wedding."

"Awesome! When?"

Charlie told her our plans, and she was ecstatic. Amanda was surprised that we planned to pull a wedding and reception together in just a few days, but her exuberance was delightful. By then, all of the dining room guests were looking at us.

In a loud, celebratory voice, Amanda proudly announced to everyone, "We have exciting news. Vickie's going to marry my grandfather on Saturday morning at 11:00 a.m. in the chapel. Please join us on this happy occasion!" We saved a lot of money on invitations.

"Who's going to be your bridesmaid?" Amanda asked.

"I was hoping you would," I said. "And GP would like your dad to be best man."

"Cool." Amanda gave us both a hug before dancing back to the kitchen.

"Guess she's happy about it," Charlie said with a chuckle.

"We all are," Steve agreed.

^^^

After supper, I called Father Jim. He said he'd love to officiate at our wedding. After chatting about a few details, he told us that he'd meet with us on Friday evening to begin the official process. Since I'm not Catholic, we won't have a Mass; just the exchange of vows.

Charlie and I took a walk to Betty's poustinia so I could tell her our good news. She was reading on her front porch when we arrived.

Charlie sat on the stoop, while I plopped into the other rocking chair. After filling her in with everything we knew at this point, Betty got over her initial shock and wished us much joy and happiness.

"I always knew that you were meant to be together," she said. "It took you both long enough to realize it."

"We're not wasting any more time," I agreed.

Betty laughed. "That's for sure! Have you decided where the honeymoon's going to be?"

"We haven't talked about that, yet, but I think I'd prefer to wait. What do you think, Charlie?"

"It's up to you," he said.

"You're a smart man," Betty said with a wink to Charlie. "You already know that Vicki likes to call the shots."

"Charlie knows quite well how to call the shots," I said. "It was his idea to have the wedding this weekend."

"You said you didn't want to wait," Charlie reminded me. "It just made sense to have it while our friends are already here."

"Perfectly natural," Betty said, "though most people take time to plan. Will you be going to your place after the reception, Vicki?"

I looked at Charlie. He nodded his approval.

"We didn't talk about that either," I said with a giggle. "But it's the best option. We're meeting with Sister Marian on Friday afternoon to discuss plans for a home here. Once we know how the Sisters want to proceed, we'll have a better grasp of our own direction."

Betty offered to help us with the wedding, but I told her that I wasn't even sure exactly what we needed to do. My brain was reeling at this point. Betty said she understood. She couldn't imagine how I was able to remain so calm.

Before we left, I made certain she knew that Charlie and I wanted her to be with us on Saturday morning. Betty promised to come to my cabin bright and early to help with last minute preparations.

As we sauntered back to my cabin, I said to Charlie, "You OK with going to my house for a while?"

"I was thinking that Leon might need my help for next week's harvest. But Steve's leaving on Saturday, so I won't have a place to bunk here."

"You're right," I said. "We'll have to figure that out."

"I'm kicking myself for leaving my car with Tony," Charlie said, shaking his head. "If I had transportation, I could go back and forth from your place."

"Our place," I said.

"Right."

"Maybe Amanda could lend you her car, until you can get yours. Hers is just parked in the lot."

"That could work. I'll ask her. What's the story about a home here?"

"The nuns were talking about building a house for us on the property. Over by where the farm's going to be. But I'm not really comfortable about that."

"Why not?"

"First of all, home construction takes a long time. Winter will be upon us before you know it. And secondly, you'll need a place to stay in order to oversee renovations on JW's barn until I can wrap things up at my firm."

"You want me to see if I can rent us a place in town?"

"What do you think about us buying a modular home?" I asked. "One of the gals at work got one, and it was completed in just a few months. I was impressed with how nice it was. Maybe we could buy a piece of land from the nuns since they're going to sell some off anyway. Then, we put the modular home on it, and the place will be ours."

"Works for me," Charlie said. "I'd like to see the property lines for the estate to get a better idea of where the barn is. You know, in respect to where we'd want to put the house."

"Me, too."

"That's public information," Charlie said. "We could stop at the courthouse on the way home from the mall tomorrow. That'd be easier than getting the nuns to try to find the deed to the estate."

After Charlie said good-night, I sat on the porch with a cup of tea. I realized that I was beyond exhausted. I worked the harvest, got engaged, picked up a marriage license, planned a wedding, and decided to build a new home.

I chuckled to myself that Betty was right. I'll have plenty of tales to tell my future great-grandkids.

Chapter 48

I called Myra early Thursday morning to tell her my news. Despite the short notice, I was hoping she'd be able to attend our wedding. To say the least, she was rather surprised and wanted to hear all of the particulars. I filled her in as quickly as possible since I knew Charlie would be at my door any moment. In the end, Myra said she'd see if Kate might be able to bring her to the monastery before the festivities on Saturday.

After shopping for the rings and wedding outfits, Charlie and I got a copy of the monastery deed at the county courthouse. Then we spent the greater part of Thursday adding flesh to my original proposal to the Sisters. We worked at the desk in my cabin, only taking a break on the front porch to eat sandwiches we had brought back for supper.

Charlie and I added the final touches to our presentation on Friday morning. It felt good to know that I wouldn't have to stammer some incomprehensible response when folks asked us about our plans. We just needed Sister Marian's approval.

Marian greeted us at the door when we arrived for our meeting, and welcomed us to the community room. This time, only Sister Cathy was present, because she was in charge of the purse strings. That's what Marian stated, which brought a round of laughter.

The Sisters presented us with the cost of facilities' rental and catering for the wedding. It was actually quite reasonable. Marian also reminded us that we'd want to offer a stipend to Father Jim for his services as minister. Tips for the luncheon servers, as well as the cost to purchase a simple wedding cake, had been included in the catering fee.

Marian asked if we'd had time to consider any details for the start of my new role as managing director. Charlie opened the folder with our extensive notes. It was evident that we were prepared.

"The first item we'd like to discuss," Charlie noted, "is our housing. We were able to take a look at the property lines by getting a copy of your deed."

Charlie pulled out the deed, showing the Sisters where we approximated that the old barn is located. He indicated the area we thought might be a good location for the start-up of the farm.

"We'll need to get an engineer," he added, "but we think that the entrance could be located here." He pointed to a spot on the site line map. "We'd like to purchase an acre of land here, with our driveway coming off the main farm road."

"You don't need to purchase the land for your home," Marian said. "We've planned for that."

"We appreciate your thoughtfulness," I replied, "but I'd feel more comfortable if we bought the land from you. We'd like to buy our own modular home to put within this copse of trees. It's not on a flood plain, but we'd be able to see the creek from the front, and the pasture from the rear of the house."

"Why do you want a modular home?" Cathy asked.

"We'd like to get started as soon as possible, based on your earlier suggestion," I said. "Once we have a home on-site, Charlie can oversee the restoration of JW's barn and supervise volunteers in building fences for the pastures."

"That makes sense," Marian agreed, nodding her head.

"My plan is to give notice to my firm on Monday," I said. "I'd like to stay until September 30, as that will be my 40-year anniversary. The bonus I'll receive will help support us during our initial weeks at *Rock Creek Farm*."

"We told you that we have our community's approval to provide you a substantial salary," Cathy reminded us.

"I think we can manage without it initially," I said, "if I can get the grant I've been working on. Regardless, I'll put my home on the market right away. The equity in my house should provide us the ability to purchase the land and modular home. Charlie's pretty handy, so he can do some minor upgrades to make my place more attractive to a buyer."

"This is amazing," Marian said. "When would you start?"

"Technically, October 1," I said. "Obviously, it all depends on many factors, such as when our home will be ready and when my house sells. Regardless, we're proposing that Leon begin clearing the woods where JW's machine barn is located. Charlie can help him on weekends, once he has a place to stay."

"The cultural tour circuit is pretty popular around here in the fall," Charlie said. "If Leon and I can get the roof of the old barn fixed, Vicki can get the Smithfield's barn and still on their docket. We'd like to extend the tour through the mansion's basement because we think it'd be good advertisement for the B&B and restaurant. Of course, that's up to you."

"We concur," Marian said. "Who'd give the tours?"

"That, too, is up to you," Charlie replied.

"Maybe one of you could be the tour guide while we get started," Marian said. "In time, Sister Cathy might like to conduct tours since she's shown so much interest in the history of the mansion."

"I'll think about it," Cathy stated. "Did you consider any programming for kids? Cheryl said she'd like to be involved with that."

"After I finish the grant for a director, I'll work on one for educational programs," I noted. "In addition, if we can get some fencing done before the ground freezes, we could have crops planted in early spring. Maybe even purchase a few animals."

"The two of you are a force to be reckoned with," Cathy said with a chuckle. "Good thing you're both in cahoots."

"Do you approve our plan?" Charlie asked.

Cathy gave a thumbs up. Marian nodded her agreement. "Completely," she said.

"Then we'll begin to put all of this into play on Monday," I said. "Charlie's going to borrow Amanda's car so he can be back next week to help Leon with the grape harvest."

"No honeymoon?" Cathy asked.

"Not yet. We're really excited to get started. After supper, we'll meet with Father Jim to make sure everything's set for our wedding."

Marian and Cathy had similar expressions on their faces, a combination of wonder and admiration. Charlie beamed. He put his arm around my shoulder, a comforting gesture which I relished.

"Everything will be perfect," Marian stated emphatically. "We'll make sure of it."

Chapter 49

A magnificent sunrise on Saturday morning matched the weather prediction of a warm and sunny day. Still in my robe, I brought my tea to the front porch of the cabin and reflected on the changes to my life that had already been set in motion. I wasn't having second thoughts. It was one of those moments, though, that I just needed to take a deep breath, close my eyes, and leap.

The depth of my love for Charlie was indisputable, and it began with the fact that he had become such a wonderful friend. We were different in many ways, but we had similar ideas. Put us together, and great things happened.

My reverie was interrupted when Betty appeared on the path to my poustinia with her mug and a coffee cake. She wasn't kidding when she said she'd be here bright and early. Guess she knew I'd be grateful for some company. Betty sat in the other rocking chair, and put the Entenmann's box on the little table. She, too, was in her robe and slippers.

"I brought my own cup of coffee. I need some kick in the morning. You doing OK?"

"I'm great. I was just thinking about how significant it is that I'm marrying such a dear friend. Don't think that this will diminish the friendship that you and I share. It's just different."

"I know what you mean," Betty said. "John was my best friend, but we needed others to balance our good marriage. It'll be the same for you and Charlie."

I nodded my agreement. It was nice to have someone at the same stage of life with whom I could share my thoughts. This was all so new to me. I couldn't imagine trying to handle it alone.

While we were chatting, Betty asked about yesterday's meeting with Marian and Cathy. Elatedly, I said that everything Charlie and I proposed was approved. Of course, other emotions were crowding my head. "I think I'm more nervous about giving notice at work than anything else."

"Jitters are understandable, given that you've been at the publishing firm your entire adult life. You have a lot of changes going on in your life."

"As much as I loved my job," I said, "I knew it was time to move on. I thought it would be to retirement, not a new position. Regardless, I'll be able to do the things I enjoy while building this venture for the Sisters. It's exciting to me."

"You'll probably conduct plenty of interviews as you hire future staff," Betty noted.

"Exactly. I just have to realize that it's going to take time to get all the pieces to fit."

"You're good with the puzzle part. Taking time, not so much."

"I guess I can be a little obsessive," I said with a chuckle.

"As I always say, like a dog with a bone. Tell me more about the house you're going to build."

I explained that Charlie and I found a business not too far from the monastery that sold modular homes. Actually, Jeff had located it using his cell phone last night when we chatted with him and Kim in the sitting room. We all agreed that the pictures and floorplans looked amazing.

"How many bedrooms?"

"Three bedrooms, two baths. The one we thought would be best included a beautiful front porch and a sunroom off the back of the house. The basic house can be ready for occupancy in less than two months."

"Sounds perfect."

"We're going to stop at the showroom on our way home so we can get our order placed as soon as possible."

"You going to have a basement?"

"No, we want one floor. Kind of like aging in place, if you know what I mean. Eventually, Charlie can build a workshop out back. We'd also like a garage, but that can be added later."

Betty agreed that our plans would serve us well into the future. Glancing at her watch, she reminded me that we also had more imminent plans and it was time to get moving. Breakfast was first on the agenda. Laughing, I knew that was my cue to get a knife and plates for the coffee cake.

When I returned, Betty said, "You know, I honestly can't believe how much you've accomplished in three days."

"That's what happens when Charlie and I put our heads together," I said, handing her the knife. "Still, we couldn't have managed it all by ourselves. Everyone's been so helpful. I don't need to do a thing today except look beautiful."

"And I'm here to assist you with that. It won't be easy, but I'll do the best I can." We both giggled like schoolgirls getting ready for the prom.

As Betty was slicing the coffee cake, she asked about the reception. I told her that Amanda was taking care of everything, with Joe's help, of course. Since Charlie and I had wanted to keep it simple, she decided to serve tea sandwiches and finger food. The Sisters ordered a wedding cake from the bakery.

"Aren't Amanda and Joe going to want to take part in the festivities? And what about Kate?"

"Joe asked some of his buddies from the diner to serve as waiters. Kate will make the drive to get her grandmother, Myra. So, the young chefs won't have to work. Joe told me not to worry. Everything's under control."

Betty agreed that all the wheels were set in motion. She suggested that I get my shower and begin to get dressed. She'd do the same at her cabin, and be back to do my makeup.

As she departed, I knew there was no turning back now. Nervous or not, I was ready. Let's get to this wedding.

Chapter 50

Sister Julie arrived at my cabin in the golf cart to bring Betty and me to the chapel. I reminded myself that this would be among the funniest memories to tell my future great-grandkids. Who needs a limousine when a golf cart's readily available?

Amanda was waiting my arrival, and gave her approval of my outfit. I had purchased a simple white sheath dress that I could wear for other occasions, and bought a matching pair of heels. She presented me with a pretty floral corsage and pinned it near my left shoulder. Amanda whispered that Betty had done a remarkable job on my makeup. I'm pretty sure that was meant to be a compliment.

I noticed that Charlie and Steve were waiting at the front of the chapel, while most of the guests were seated. Kate, her parents, and Myra were with Joe in the second row of pews. Jeff and Kim sat with Betty, Hannah, and a few of the Sisters in front of them. Intermingled were Leon, a couple of Charlie's buddies from the firehouse, Sister Cathy, and Sister Cheryl. Julie slipped in to sit with them. Even some of the infirmary Sisters were watching from the balcony.

Father Jim joined Amanda and me at the side entrance of the chapel and told us that we were ready to proceed. We'd had a brief rehearsal last evening, so Charlie and I were prepared for what to expect. Father Jim would go to the altar; Charlie and Steve would stand with him there. Amanda would walk ahead of me from the back of chapel, then she and her dad would sit on chairs arranged to the side of the altar. Father Jim would greet us, then Charlie and I would take seats on the other side of the altar until it was time for the exchange of vows.

When everyone was in place, one of the Sisters began playing the organ. I kept my eyes on Charlie as I walked down the aisle. He looked very dapper in his new suit, and prouder than a peacock. When I met up with him, we joined hands and sat in our appointed seats.

Father Jim said some opening prayers, and Sister Marian gave the first reading from the Old Testament. After a few more prayers, Sister Dolores read a passage from the New Testament. They seemed to know what they were doing.

After reading the gospel, Father Jim asked everyone to be seated as he had a few words to say. He told the story of the wedding at Cana, which was fitting, he explained, since it was the first recorded miracle of Jesus, who turned water into wine.

"You might wonder what this has to do with Vicki and Charlie," he said, "but I believe it relates quite well. Let me tell you why."

Father Jim likened the large jars of water to all of us. Just ordinary people. Like the pottery, some of us might have seen better days. Others might be a little cracked. Regardless of our origin, we were the vessels of transformation.

"The Sisters have a mission," he continued, gazing at each person in the congregation. "They strive to bring God's message to those they meet. They've provided simple dwellings for us to find solitude and peace. Charlie was the first to experience the transformative power of healing when he assisted Sister Tony with the planning and building of the poustinias. The rest of us have also been touched. Each person who has been here at the monastery leaves with a gift. Probably not visible or tangible. Perhaps something already present within themselves, but not recognized. When Vicki arrived, she was searching for answers. She didn't solve her own dilemma; she added to the Sisters' quandary."

Everyone laughed; Charlie squeezed my hand. I thought how true it was that the Sisters had a way of opening our spirits without being intrusive.

Father Jim continued. "Jesus told the servants to fill the jugs with water. Just regular water. When their glasses were refreshed, the wedding guests commented that usually the best wine was served first. Instead the groom saved the best for last. Charlie and Vicki took the long road to stand before us today. They have both been transformed individually, and that change has had a ripple effect on all of us. We're all better for having associated with them, for calling them our friends. Just as with the wedding at Cana, we're here to celebrate the best. We're honored that two ordinary people have decided to join their talents together, to share their gifts, and to assist the Sisters in expanding their mission. We're blessed to witness their vows."

I had tears in my eyes by the end of the homily. I certainly didn't see myself as being like the wine at Cana, but I recognized how much Charlie and I have been transformed. Not through anything we did ourselves, but by virtue of interacting with the Sisters and those we've met at the Monastery of St. Carmella.

Charlie and I stood to join Father Jim at the altar. Steve moved to Charlie's right side; Amanda was at my left. Charlie and I recited our vows, and Steve handed Charlie the ring. "With this ring, I thee wed," Charlie said with deep emotion.

Father Jim finalized the ceremony. "I now pronounce you man and wife. You may kiss the bride."

It was a really nice kiss, if I may say so myself.

Chapter 51

I hugged and kissed each of our guests as Charlie and I made our way down the aisle and out the side door. Joe insisted that we pose for wedding photos, then Amanda led us to the beautifully decorated dining room. What I didn't expect was a side table arranged with gifts. Lots of them.

Charlie and I greeted our guests, while Amanda directed them to seat themselves at the tables of their choice. A tray of assorted tea sandwiches was at the center of each table. A few of Joe's buddies, serving as waiters, began pouring champagne. Others offered guests a variety of hors d'oeuvres.

Joe directed Charlie and me to take our places at the table of honor. We were pleased that the special people in our lives were with us. Steve, Amanda, and Hannah were to Charlie's left, while Betty, Father Jim, and Joe were to my right.

"Where'd we get the bottles of champagne?" I whispered to Charlie.

"Sister Tony and the Sisters in St. Louis sent them as a wedding gift. I told you she gave her blessing."

"That was thoughtful of them," I said. "Nice touch."

When everyone was settled, Steve clinked his glass and stood to give a toast. I knew he'd be a little nervous to be in the limelight, but Hannah's encouraging smile gave him support.

"It's not every day that a son has the opportunity to serve as best man at his father's wedding. I'm honored to present a toast in honor of Vicki and my dad, Charlie. I have to admit, I had to get help from the Bible. I mean, really, we're at a monastery."

Once the laughter died down, Steve was more relaxed. I had no idea what he planned to say, but it was a good start.

"So, this is what I found," Steve continued. "St. Paul told the Corinthians, 'Love never gives up, never loses faith, is always hopeful, and endures through every circumstance.' I guess it took a long time for my dad and Vicki to know that they were meant to be together. Lucky for us, love prevailed. We're here to celebrate with you on your special day, and to wish you a long and happy marriage. Cheers!"

"Hear, hear!" Charlie exclaimed. He and I took a sip of our champagne.

Amanda stood and raised her glass. "I can't let my father get the best of me, despite what Father Jim said in the ceremony. My grandfather and Vicki may have tied the knot before Joe and I did, but we beat them to the engagement. I just want to say, it took you two a long time to get it together, but when you did, you really moved fast. Seriously, I can't think of anything better than to have Vicki as the grandmother I always wanted. Great choice, GP!"

Jeff called out from the crowd, "What are you going to call Vicki? GM?"

"She'll always be Vicki to me," Amanda said, giving me a huge smile. "She's the best friend I'll ever have."

Charlie squeezed my hand as my eyes misted. I mouthed a thank you before raising my glass. Amanda nodded, then gave me a hug. It was a very touching moment.

After we ate, everyone mingled from table to table. This was why Charlie and I had wanted a small wedding. We wanted time to enjoy talking with each of our dear friends. Before he left to chat with the Sisters and Leon, I made sure to thank Father Jim for such a memorable ceremony. He said he'd been honored to participate, wishing both of us many happy years together.

I waved Myra over, telling her how happy I was that she had been able to come on such short notice. With a chuckle, she said that Harvey hadn't been too pleased about her leaving him alone for the day, but he settled himself to snooze on the sofa.

"He'll be fine," I said. "And I'll pick him up tonight. Charlie and I should arrive before dark. I'm so glad that Kate brought her parents as well."

"Yeah. She wanted them to meet the Sisters."

I glanced in their direction, observing that Kate and her parents were deep in conversation with Marian and Cheryl. For some reason, it made me wonder if they were offering Kate a full-time job.

"What's that all about?" I asked Myra.

"I'm not at liberty to discuss it yet. I'll tell you later."

I didn't get a chance to respond because Joe wanted to take more photos. Before I knew it, Charlie and I were invited to cut the cake. I looked for Amanda to see if she wanted to assist, but she was nowhere to be found. Joe told me that she and Kate were in the kitchen. He didn't seem very happy about it.

Charlie was a perfect gentleman as we gave each other a bite of cake. Everyone applauded, and the waiters began to distribute a piece to each guest. Before we sat down again, I suggested to Charlie that we should say a few words.

I clinked my glass for attention. "Charlie and I want to thank each of you for sharing in this very special day," I said. "I know we didn't give you much notice, but we're so grateful for your presence, as well as your friendship. Father Jim was right that our lives are intermingled because of our experiences at the Monastery of St. Carmella. I don't think we've been transformed because we stayed in a rustic cabin in the woods. I believe that sharing in the mission of the Sisters, and being open to new beginnings, has been a blessing for each of us."

I nudged Charlie, urging him to say something. "I agree with Vicki," he said. "We're glad you could be with us today."

"You going to be here to pick the grapes this week?" Leon asked.

"I'll be here to help you, Leon," Charlie said. He looked at me as he continued. "Vicki and I are going home for a few days, then I'll be back for the harvest."

"Most of you know that I'll be managing *Rock Creek Farm* in just over a month," I added. "We plan to have a small working farm and offer educational programs, so we'll need a lot of help to get started. Do you think you can find us some volunteers, Father?"

"Plenty of them," he said, nodding his head in agreement. "Leon can be in charge."

"Where're you going to live?" Myra asked.

"Charlie and I are building a home overlooking the farm. He'll be overseeing the construction, and we'll be moving in as soon as it's ready."

Amanda and Kate joined the group at that moment and Amanda said, "You're not the only one moving to this place."

Everyone turned to Amanda. She looked at Kate. Kate said simply, "I'm going to be a Sister."

I was absolutely floored. I honestly never expected such news. We all applauded, then laughed, as Amanda said, "Geez, Kate's going to be a nun. Who'd believe it?"

Turning to Myra, I whispered, "Is she Catholic?"

"Her mother is, and Kate was baptized as an infant. I was surprised when she told us her plans because she was never very religious."

"What about college?" I asked.

"She'll still attend college, but she'll be considered an aspirant for this next year."

"What's that mean?"

"I'm not sure. Something about living at the monastery on weekends and school breaks, then she'll have a better idea of what's involved in being a nun. When they think she's ready, the Sisters will accept her as a postulant. That's what they call the first step in training."

I meandered over to Amanda. "You OK about Kate?" I whispered.

"I was upset when she first told me. Maybe because I was so surprised. You know what I'm saying? I mean, like, she likes guys. She wanted to get married and have babies. We used to talk about it all the time."

"She might just want to see what it's like to be a nun."

"No, she's serious. We had a heart-to-heart in the kitchen. At first, I thought she was being a little kooky. But, you know what? She's going to be a really cool nun."

Chapter 52

Guests slowly began to depart, each stopping by for final good wishes. Charlie and I thanked his buddies at the fire station for coming. We were pleased to see how friendly they had been to Leon, even inviting him to call Bingo on Friday nights. We said farewell to Jeff and Kim. They planned to spend the afternoon at the lake before their departure.

Kate's parents left with Myra. I promised to continue our conversation later when I picked up Harvey. Myra and I still had a lot to talk about. Betty hugged me, saying she'd call during the week.

Sister Dolores left to open the gift shop in case anyone wanted to browse, while Sister Julie transported guests to their cars in the golf cart. Sister Cheryl directed the waiters for clean-up and re-setting the table for dinner service.

Steve and Hannah told us how much they enjoyed being with us to celebrate. In one voice, Charlie and I said we wouldn't have had it any other way. We made sure they knew we wanted them to be frequent visitors to our home.

Smiling, Steve nodded his agreement. "And, by the way, Amanda told me this morning how much she likes Hannah."

"What's not to like?" I remarked with a wink to Hannah. "But I'm sure it's a relief to you both."

"You can't imagine. She even said, 'she's a keeper, dad.'"

"You were wise to let them get to know each other better. Coming to the B&B was the best thing you could have done."

"Father Jim was right, you know."

"How so?"

"This place is transformative."

"That it is, Steve. That it is."

^^^

Charlie and Joe went to get my car and Amanda's car from the parking lot. When they pulled up to the front entrance, we began carrying out the wedding gifts, packing them into the trunks and back seats. Our suitcases had already been loaded before the ceremony. It made me laugh to see that someone, perhaps by the name of Amanda, had decorated both cars with tin cans and signs. One read, "Just married." The other, "Just married, too."

Charlie and I were finally ready for our departure. Sister Marian, Sister Cathy, and Father Jim stood by the ornate door under the *porte couchère*. I gazed at the beautiful stonework on the mansion behind them. Sunlight was reflected off the stained glass windows on the second floor.

I thought about JW Smithfield and his wife, Hildegarde, perhaps having stood in the exact location as they bid farewell to their distinguished guests. None of those visitors would have suspected that a secret passageway to an illegal enterprise was located almost directly under their feet. If Sister Cathy hadn't been curious to gather information about the benefactors who had bequeathed their estate to the Sisters, we'd have been none the wiser either.

"You'll be back soon," Marian said. "We'll be praying that that your home sells quickly."

"I'll bring some volunteers from the shelter," Father Jim promised. "We can help Leon clear the trees around JW's barn.

Once he and Charlie get the roof repaired, it'll be ready for you to weave your magic."

"Nothing magical about what I do," I said.

"Don't you believe it," Charlie and Father Jim responded in one voice. Everyone else add their two cents until I laughingly called a halt.

"Don't forget to give me a buzz if you need any financial information when you're working on a grant," Sister Cathy said. "Believe it or not, I actually like putting the numbers together."

I promised, before thanking Amanda, Joe, and Kate for all they had done to make our wedding reception so special. They had been standing by the cars, impatiently waiting for us to stop all the small talk.

"We're just happy that everything worked out," Amanda said with a broad grin, leaning forward to kiss my cheek.

"GP and I love you."

"Love you, too. But if you two don't hurry up and leave, we won't have much time at the lake this afternoon."

"I forgot to ask you," I said, opening the car door. "When's your wedding going to be?"

"You think we've had time to figure that out yet?"

"I can give you some pointers on wedding planning," I teased.

"Yeah, right."

"I just had a brainstorm," I said. "Kate will be the newest Sister at the monastery. We can put her in charge of making the goat cheese."

"Awesome," Kate replied. She looked at Sister Marian for affirmation.

"Not a bad idea," Marian said with a chuckle. "Now get out of here so these guys get a break before dinner service."

I got into the driver's seat of my car. Charlie planned to follow me in Amanda's car. I turned to him and said, "You know what? I don't want to leave."

"We'll be back before you know it."

As I pulled away, I heard Amanda say, "Drive carefully, GP. They're the only wheels I've got."

ABOUT THE AUTHOR

Kathleen McKee is an accomplished educator and gifted writer with a talent for bringing characters to life. Her heart-warming stories and their settings are drawn from memories of people she has met and places she has experienced.

Kathleen crafts narratives that are uplifting and moving, with a touch of whimsy, mystery, and history. She likes to include women who are strong, generous, compassionate, and capable.

The monastery in *Joyful Encounters* is reminiscent of the Drexel Mansion, built by George W. Childs 1891. It was purchased by the Sisters of IHM in the late 1940's to provide accommodations for their boarding school for boys. And yes, there was a vintage bowling alley in the basement.

Kathleen currently lives in Southeast Pennsylvania. You'll find her there working on her next novel. Visit her website at: https://kathleen-mckee.com/

32841574R00141

Made in the USA
Middletown, DE
10 January 2019